ROBERT W

The Haunting of
Chas McGill

and other stories

**MACMILLAN
CHILDREN'S BOOKS**

First published 1983 by Macmillan Children's Books

This edition published 1995 by Macmillan Children's Books
a division of Macmillan Publishers Ltd
25 Eccleston Place London SW1W 9NF
and Basingstoke

Associated companies throughout the world

ISBN 0 330 34065 4

This collection © Robert Westall 1983

The Haunting of Chas McGill © Robert Westall 1981
Almost a Ghost Story © Robert Westall 1983
The Vacancy © Robert Westall 1983
The Night Out © Robert Westall 1980
The Creatures in the House © Robert Westall 1980
Sea-coal © Robert Westall 1982
The Dracula Tour © Robert Westall 1983
A Walk on the Wild Side © Robert Westall 1983

The Haunting of Chas McGill first published in GHOST
AFTER GHOST: Kestrel, 1982. *The Night Out* first
published in LOVE YOU, HATE YOU, JUST DON'T
KNOW: Evans Bros, 1980. *The Creatures in the House*
first published in YOU CAN'T KEEP OUT THE
DARKNESS: Bodley Head, 1980. *Sea-coal* first published
in SCHOOL'S O.K.: Evans Bros, 1982.

The right of Robert Westall to be identified as the
author of this work has been asserted by him in accordance
with the Copyright, Designs and Patents Act 1988.

A CIP catalogue record for this book is available from
the British Library

Phototypeset by Intype, London
Printed by Mackays of Chatham PLC, Kent

For Felicity, who simply conjured this book out of
the air.

Contents

The Haunting of Chas McGill

THE day war broke out, Chas McGill went up in the world.

What a Sunday morning! Clustering round the radio at eleven o'clock, all hollow-bellied like the end of an England–Australia Test. Only this was the England–Germany Test. He had his score-cards all ready, pinned on his bedroom wall: number of German tanks destroyed; number of German planes shot down; number of German ships sunk.

The Prime Minister's voice, finally crackling over the air, seemed to Chas a total disaster. Mr Chamberlain *regretted* that a state of war now existed between England and Germany. Worse, he bleated like a sheep; or the sort of kid who, challenged in the playground, backs into a corner with his hands in front of his face and threatens to tell his Dad on you. Why didn't he threaten to kick Hitler's teeth in? Chas hoped Hitler wasn't listening, or there'd soon be trouble . . .

Immediately, the air-raid sirens went.

German bombers. Chas closed his eyes and remembered the cinema newsreels from Spain. Skies thick with black crosses, from which endless streams of tiny bombs fell. Endless as the streams of refugee women scurrying through the shattered houses, all wearing headscarves and ankle-socks. Rows of dead kids laid out on the shattered brickwork like broken-stick dolls with glass eyes. (He always shut his eyes at that point, but *had* to peep.) And the German bomber-pilots, hardly human in tight black leather flying-helmets, laughing and slapping each other on the back and busting open bottles of champagne and spraying each other . . .

He opened his eyes again. Through his bedroom window the grass of the Square still dreamed in sunlight. Happy ignorant sparrows, excused the war, were busy pecking their breakfast from the steaming pile of manure left by the Co-op milkhorse. The sky remained clear and blue; not a Spitfire in sight.

Chas wondered what he ought to *do*? Turn off the gas and electric? With Mam in the middle of Sunday dinner, that'd be more dangerous than any air-raid. His eye fell on his teddy-bear, sitting on top of a pile of toys in the corner. He hadn't given Ted a glance in years. Now, Ted stared at him appealingly. There'd been teddy-bears in the Spanish newsreels too; the newsreels were particularly keen on teddy-bears split from chin to crotch, with all their stuffing spilling out. Headless teddy-bears, legless teddy bears . . . Making sure no one was watching, he grabbed Ted and shoved him under the bed to safety.

Not a moment too soon. Mam came in, drying her sudsy hands.

'Anything happening out front? Nothing happening out the back.' She made it sound like they were waiting for a carnival with a brass band, or something. She peered intently out of the window.

2

'There's an air-raid warden.'

'It's only old Jimmy Green.'

'*Mr* Green to you. Well, he wrote to the Air Raid Precautions yesterday, offering his services, so I expect he thinks he's got to do his bit.'

Jimmy was wearing his best blue suit; though whether in honour of the war, or only because it was Sunday, Chas couldn't tell. But he was wearing all his medals from the Great War, and his gas-mask in a cardboard box, hanging on a piece of string across his chest. His chest was pushed well out, and he was marching round the Square, swinging his arms like the Coldstream guardsman he'd once been.

'I'll bet he's got Hitler scared stiff.'

'If he sounds his rattle,' said Mam, 'put your gas-mask on.'

'He hasn't *got* a rattle.'

'Well, that's what it says in the papers. An' if he blows his whistle, we have to go down the air-raid shelter.'

Chas bleakly surveyed the Anderson shelter, lying in pieces all over the front lawn, where it had been dumped by council workmen yesterday. It might do the worms a bit of good . . .

'Who's that?'

Jimmy had been joined by a more important air-raid warden. So important he actually had a black steel helmet with a white 'W' on the front. Jimmy pointed to a mad happy dog who, finding the empty world much to his liking, was chasing its tail all over the Square. The important warden consulted a little brown book, and obviously decided the dog was a threat to National Security. They made a prolonged and hopeless attempt to catch the dog, who loved it.

'The Germans are dropping them Alsatians by parachute,' said Chas. 'To annoy the wardens.'

That earned a clout. 'Stop spreading rumours and causing despondency. They can put you in prison for that!'

Chas wondered about prison; prisons had thick walls and concrete ceilings, at least in the movies. Definitely bomb-proof . . .

But a third figure had emerged into the Square. An immensely stocky lady in a flowered hat. A cigarette thrust from her mouth and two laden shopping bags hung from each hand. She was moving fast, and panting through her cigarette; the effect was of a small but powerful steam-locomotive. The very sight of her convinced Chas that the newsreels from Spain were no more real than Marlene Dietrich in *Destry Rides Again*. Bloody ridiculous.

She made the wardens look pretty ridiculous, too, as they ran one each side of her, gesticulating fiercely.

'Get out of me way, Arthur Dunhill, an' tek that bloody silly hat off. Ye look like something out of a fancy-dress ball. Aah divvent care if they hev made ye Chief Warden. Aah remember ye as a snotty-nosed kid being dragged up twelve-in-two-rooms in over Hudson Street. If ye think that snivelling gyet Hitler can stop me performin' me natural functions on a Sunday morning ye're very much mistaken . . .'

'It's your Nana,' said Mam, superfluously but with much relief. Next minute, Nana was sitting in the kitchen, sweating cobs and securely entrenched among her many shopping-bags.

'Let me get me breath. Well, she's done it now. Tempy. She's *really* done it.'

'It wasn't Tempy,' said Chas. 'It was Hitler.'

'Aah'll cross his bridge when aah come to it. You know what Tempy's done? Evaccyated all her school to Keswick, and we've all got to go and live at The Elms as caretakers.'

Chas gave an inward screech of agony. Tempy gone to Keswick meant the loss of ten shillings a term. Thirty bob a year. How many Dinky toys would that buy?

War might be hell, but thirty shillings was serious.

The siren suddenly sounded the all-clear.

Mam let Chas go out and watch for the taxi in the blackout. The blackout was a flop. It just wasn't black. True, the street-lamps weren't lit, and every house window carefully curtained. But the longer he stood there, the brighter the sky grew, until it seemed as bright as day.

He'd hauled the two big suitcases out of the house, with a lot of sweat. He stood between them, ready to duck in case a low-flying Messerschmitt 109 took advantage of the lack of blackout to strafe the Square. Machine-gun bullets throwing up mounds of earth, like in *Hell's Angels* starring Ben Lyon. He wondered if the suitcases would stop a bullet. They seemed full of insurance-books and all fifteen pairs of Mam's apricot-coloured knickers. Still, in war, one had to take risks . . .

The taxi jerked into the Square at ten miles an hour, and pulled up some distance away.

'Number eighteen?' shouted the driver querulously. 'Can't see a bloody thing.' No wonder. He had covered his windscreen with crosses of sticky-tape to protect it against bomb-blast, and peered through like a spider out of its web.

'Get on, ye daft bugger,' shouted Nana from the back. 'Ah cud drive better wi' me backside.' Granda, totally buried beside her in a mound of blankets, travelling rugs, overcoats and mufflers for his chest, coughed prolonged agreement.

It was a strange journey to The Elms. Chas had to sit on the suitcases, with what felt like Nana's wash-day-mangle sticking in his ribs.

'I shouldn't have left the house empty like that,' wailed Mam. 'There'll be burglars an' who's going to water the tomatoes?'

'You coulda left a note asking the burglars to do it,' said Chas. It was too dark and jam-packed in the taxi for any danger of a clout.

'Ye'll be safer at The Elms hinny,' said Nana. 'Now ye haven't got a man to put a steadyin' hand to you.'*

'She's got *me*,' said Chas.

'God love yer – a real grown man. 'Spect ye'll be j'ining up in the Army soon as ye're twelve.'

'Aah j'ined up at fourteen,' said Granda. 'To fight the Boers. Fourteen years, seven months, six days. Aah gave a false birthday.'

'Much good it's done you since,' said Nana, 'wi' that gassing they gave you at Wipers.'

'That wasn't the Boers,' said Chas helpfully, 'that was the Germans.'

*Mr McGill joined the RAF in 1938, during the Munich Crisis, but was discharged with flat feet in the winter of 1939, and was at home during the night blitz of 1940–1, as readers of *The Machine-Gunners* will know.

6

Granda embarked on a bout of coughing, longer and more complicated than 'God Save the King', that silenced all opposition for two miles.

'It'll be safer for the bairn,' added Nana finally. 'Good as evaccyating him. Hitler won't bomb Preston nor The Elms. He's got more respec' for his betters . . . besides, ye had to come, hinny. I can't manage that great spooky place on my own – not wi' yer Granda an' his chest.'

'Spooky?' asked Chas.

'Don't mind me,' said Nana hastily. 'That's just me manner of speakin'.'

Just then, the taxi turned a corner too sharply; outside there was a thump, and the crunch of breaking glass. 'Ah well,' said Nana philosophically, 'we won't be needing them street-lamps for the Duration. Reckon it'll be all over by Christmas, once the Navy's cut off Hitler's vitals . . .'

'Painful,' said Chas.

'Aah owe it to Tempy,' concluded Nana. 'Many a job she's pushed my way, ower the years, when yer Granda's had his chest . . .'

Chas pushed his nose against the steamed-up window of the taxi, feeling as caged as a budgie. He watched the outskirts of Garmouth fall away; a few fields, then the taxi turned wildly into the private road where the roofs of great houses peeped secretly over shrubbery and hedge and tree, and, at the end, was The Elms, Miss Temple's ancestral home and late private school and the biggest of them all.

So by bedtime, on the third of September 1939, Chas

had risen very high in the world indeed. A third-floor attic, with the wind humming in the wireless aerial that stretched between the great chimneys, and ivy leaves tapping on his window, so it sounded as if it was raining. Granda's old army greatcoat had been hung over the window for lack of curtains.

Chas didn't like it at all, even if he did have candle and matches, a rather dim torch, a book called *Deeds That Have Won the VC* and six toy pistols under his pillow. You couldn't shoot spooks with a toy pistol, he didn't feel like winning the VC, and he wanted the lav, bad.

There was a great cold white chamber-pot under the narrow servant's bed, but he'd no intention of using it. Mam would be sure to inspect the contents in the morning, and tell everyone at breakfast how his kidneys were functioning. Mam feared malfunctioning kidneys more than Stuka dive-bombers.

Finally, he gathered his courage, a pistol, his torch and his too-short dressing-gown around him, and set out to seek relief.

The dark was a trackless desert, beyond his dim torch. The wind, finding its way up through the floorboards, ballooned-up the worn passage-carpet like shifting sand-dunes. The only oases were the lightswitches, and most of them didn't work, so they were, strictly speaking, mirages. Down one narrow stair . . .

The servants' lav was tall and gaunt, like a gallows; its rusting chain hung like a hangman's noose, swaying in the draught. The seat was icy and unfriendly.

Afterwards, reluctant to go back upstairs, Chas pressed on. A slightly open door, a shaft of golden

8

light, the sweet smell of old age and illness. Granda's cough was like a blessing in the strangeness.

But he didn't go in. He didn't dislike Granda, but he didn't like him either. Granda's chest made him as strange as the pyramids of Egypt. Granda's chest was the centre of the family, around which everything else revolved. As constant as the moon. He had his good spells and his bad. His good spells, when he turned over a bit of his garden, or hung a picture on the wall, grew no better. His bad spells grew no worse.

Chas passed on, noiselessly, down another flight of stairs.

He knew where he was, now. A great oak hall, with a landing running round three sides, and a broad open staircase leading down into a dim red light. Miss Temple's study was on the right.

Miss Temple, headmistress, magistrate, city councillor of Newcastle. He knew her highly-polished shoes well; her legs, solid as table-legs in their pale silk stockings, her black headmistress's gown or her dark fur coat. He had never seen her face. It was always too high above him, too awesome. God must look like Miss Temple.

At the end of every term, ever since he had started school, Nana had taken him to see Miss Temple at The Elms. With his school report clutched in his hand. They were shown in by a housemaid called Claire, neat in black frock, white lace hat and apron. Up to Miss Temple's study. There, the polished black shoes would be waiting, standing four-square on the Turkey carpet, the fat pale solid legs above them.

A sallow plump soft hand, with dark hairs on the back, would descend into his line of vision. He would put the school report into it. Hand and report would ascend out of sight. There would be a long silence, like the Last Judgement. Then Miss Temple's voice would come floating down, deep as an angel's trumpet.

'Excellent, Charles . . . excellent.' Then she would ask him what he was going to be when he grew up; but he could never answer. The plump hand would descend again, with the report and something brown that crackled enticingly.

A ten-bob note. He would mumble thanks that didn't make sense even to himself. Then the tiny silver watch that slightly pinched the dark plum wrist would be consulted, and a gardener-chauffeur called Holmes would be summoned, to drive Miss Temple in state to Newcastle, for dinner, or a meeting of the full council, or some other godlike occasion.

It never varied. He never really breathed until he was outside again, and the air smelled of trees and grass, and not of polish and Miss Temple. Sometimes, hesitating, he would ask Nana why Miss Temple was not like anybody else. Nana always said it was because she had never married; because of something that had happened in the Great War.

And now there was another war, and Miss Temple fled to Keswick with all her pupils, and her study door locked, and outside Hitler and a great wind were loose in the world.

He crept on, past the grandfather-clock on the landing that ticked on, as indifferent to him as Holmes the chauffeur in his shiny leather gaiters. Prowled out to the back wing, where the girls' classrooms were. Searched their empty desks by torchlight, exulting spitefully over the spelling mistakes in an abandoned exercise-book. There was a knicker-blue shoe-bag hanging on the back of one classroom door. He put his hand inside with a guilty thrill, but it only contained one worn white plimsoll.

Downstairs, he got into a panic before he found the light-proof baize-covered kitchen door; thought he was cut off in the whole empty windy house, with only Granda above, immobilised and coughing.

He pushed the baize door open an inch. Cosy warmth streamed out. A roaring fire in the kitchen-range. Nana, in flowered pinny, pouring tea. Mam, still worrying on about burglars, peeling potatoes. Claire the housemaid, raffish without her lace hat, legs crossed, arms crossed, fag in her mouth, eyes squinting up against the smoke.

'Shan't be here to bother you much longer. Off to South Wales next week, working on munitions. They pay twice as much as *she* does. Holmes? Just waiting for his call-up papers for the Army. Reckons he'll spend a cushy war, driving Lord Gort about.'

Chas was tempted to go in; he loved tea and gossip. Hated the idea of the long climb back to the moaning wireless aerial and ivy-tapping windows. But Mam would only be angry . . .

He climbed. At the turn of the last stair, a landing window gave him a view of the roof and the chimneys and the row of attic windows. Six attic windows. His was the fourth . . . no, the fifth, it must be, because the fifth was dimly candle-lit. Oh God, he'd left his candle burning, and Granda's greatcoat was useless as blackout, and soon there'd be an air-raid warden shouting, 'Put that bloody light out.'

He ran, suddenly panting. Burst into his room.

It was in darkness, of course. He'd never lit his candle. And his *was* the fourth room in the corridor, the fourth shabby white door.

He ran back to the landing window. There was candle-light in the fifth window, the room next to his own. It moved, as if someone were moving about, inside the room.

Who?

Holmes, of course. Snooty Holmes. Well, Holmes's flipping blackout was Holmes's flipping business . . . Chas got back into his ice-cold bed, keeping his dressing-gown on for warmth. Put his ear to the wall. He could hear Holmes moving about, restlessly; big leather boots on uncarpeted floorboards, and a kind of continuous mournful low whistling. Miserable stuck-up bugger . . .

On that thought, he fell asleep.

Next morning, before going to the lav, he peered round his door in the direction of Holmes's. He dreaded the sneer that would cross Holmes's face, if he saw a tousle-haired kid running about in pyjamas. Nana said Holmes had once been a gentleman's gentleman, and it showed.

But there was no sign of Holmes. In fact, the whole width of the corridor, just beyond Chas's room, was blocked off by a dirty white door, unnoticed in the blackout last night. It looked like a cupboard door, too, with a keyhole high up.

Chas investigated. It *was* a cupboard; contained nothing but a worn-out broom and a battered blue tin dustpan. Then Chas forgot all about Holmes;

because the whole inside of the cupboard was papered over with old newspapers. Adverts for ladies' corsets, stiffened with the finest whalebone and fitted with the latest all-rubber suspenders. All for three shillings and elevenpence three-farthings! Better, photographs of soldiers, mud and great howitzers. And headlines.

NEW OFFENSIVE MOUNTED AT CAMBRAI

MILE OF GERMAN FIRST-LINE TRENCH TAKEN

NEW 'TANKS' IN ACTION?

Chas read on, enthralled and shivering, until Nana shouted up the stairs to ask if they were all dead up there?

As he was hurling himself into his clothes, a new thought struck him. All those old newspapers seemed to be from 1917 . . . if the cupboard had been there since then, how on earth did Holmes get into his room? He went back and rapped violently all over the inside of the cupboard. The sides were solid plaster, the plaster of the corridor walls. The back boomed hollowly, as if the corridor went on beyond it. But there was no secret door at the back; the pasted-on newspapers were intact, not a torn place anywhere.

'Are ye doing an impersonation o' a death-watch beetle? 'Cos they only eat wood, an' in that case aah'm going to throw your breakfast away.'

Even though he knew it was Nana's voice, he still nearly jumped a yard in the air.

'There's newspapers, here, with pictures of the Great War.'

'Ye've got war on the bleddy brain,' said Nana. 'Isn't one war enough for ye? Ye'll have a war on yer hands in the kitchen, too, if you don't come down for breakfast. Yer Mam's just heard on the radio that

13

school's been abolished for the Duration, an' it's raining. Aah don't know what we're going to do wi' you. Wi' all the bairns driving their Mams mad, getting under their feet, Hitler's goin' to have a walkover.'

But Chas was surprisingly good, all day. He did demand his mac and wellies, and walk round the house no less than fourteen times, staring up at the windows and counting compulsively, and getting himself soaked.

'He'll catch his death out there,' wailed Mam.

'He'll catch my hand on his lug if he comes bothering us in here. Let him bide while we're busy,' said Nana, her mouth full of pins from the blackout curtains she was sewing.

Then he came in and had his hair rubbed with a towel by Nana, until he thought his ears were being screwed off. Then he scrounged a baking-board and four drawing-pins, a sheet of shelf-lining paper, and Mam's tape-measure, and did a carefully measured plan of the whole kitchen, which everyone agreed was very fine.

'What's that great fat round thing by the kitchen sink?' asked Nana.

'You, doing the washing-up,' said Chas, already ducking so her hand missed his head by inches; she'd a heavy hand, Nana. Then, sitting up, he announced, 'I'm going to do something to help the War Effort.'

'Aye,' said Nana. 'Ye're running down to the shop for another packet of pins for me.'

'No, besides that. I'm going to make a plan of the

whole house, to help the Fire Brigade in case we get hit by an incendiary bomb . . .'

'Ye're a proper little ray o' sunshine . . .'

'Can I go into all the rooms and measure them?'

'No,' said Mam. 'Miss Temple wouldn't like it.'

'Can I, Nana,' said Chas, blatantly.

'What Tempy's eyes doesn't see, her heart won't grieve. Let the bairn be, while he's good,' said Nana, reaching for her bunch of keys from her pocket.

So, in between running down to the shop for pins, and running back to the kitchen every time there was a news broadcast, Chas roamed the veriest depths of the house.

Looking for the back stair leading up to Holmes's room.

Looking for the hidden stair leading up to Holmes's room.

Looking for the secret stair leading up to Holmes's room . . .

He searched and measured until he was blue in the face. Went outside and counted windows over and over and got himself soaked again.

No way was there a secret stair up to Holmes's room. He was pretty hungry when he came back in for tea.

Nana switched off the radio with a sniff. 'The Archbishop of Canterberry has called for a National Day of Prayer for Poland. God help the bleddy Poles, if it's come to *that*.'

'Nana,' said Chas, 'where does Holmes live?'

'*Mr* Holmes to you,' said Mam in a desperate voice. At which Holmes himself, the sneaky sod, rose in all the glory of his chauffeur's uniform and shiny leggings from the depths of the wing-chair by the fire, where he'd been downing a pint mug of tea. 'And why do you want to know that, my little man?' he said, with a know-all smirk on his face. Chas blushed from head to foot.

'Because you're in the room next to mine, an' I can't see how you get up there.' He wouldn't have blurted it out, if he hadn't been so startled.

'Well, that's where you're wrong, my little man,' said Holmes. 'I have a spacious home above the stables, with my good wife and Nancy Jane, aged nine. You must come and have tea with Nancy Jane, before I go off to serve my King and Country. She'd like that. But why on earth did you think I had a room up in the attics?'

'Because someone was moving last night, an' whistling . . .'

Holmes looked merely baffled; so did young Claire. Mam was blushing for his manners, like a beetroot. But Chas thought Nana turned as white as a sheet.

'It's only the wind in that bleddy wireless aerial. Get on wi' yer tea and stop annoying your elders an' betters . . .'

Next evening Chas pushed open the door of Granda's room, cautiously. The old man lay still, propped up on pillows, arms lying parallel, on top of the bed-clothes. He looked as if he was staring out of the window, but he might be asleep. That was one of the strange things about Granda, the amount of staring out of windows he did, when he was having one of his bad spells; and the way you could never tell if he was staring or asleep. Also the fact that his hair didn't look like hair, and his whiskers didn't look like whiskers. They looked like strange grey plants, growing out of his purply-grey skin. Or the thin roots that grow out of a turnip . . .

'Granda?'

The head turned; the eyes came back from somewhere. They tried to summon up a smile, but Chas's eyes ducked down before they managed it.

'Granda – can I borrow your brace-and-bit?'

'Aye, lad, if ye tek care of it . . . it's in the bottom drawer there, wi' the rest o' my gear . . .' The old head turned away again, eyes on a red sunset. Chas pulled out the drawer, and there was Granda's gear. Granda's gear was the only thing Chas really loved about Granda; the old man could never bear to throw anything away. Everything might come in useful . . . The drawer was full of odd brass taps, bundles of wire neatly tied up, tin toffee-boxes full of rusty screws and nails, a huge bayonet in its scabbard that Granda only used for cutting his endless supplies of hairy white string. There was the brace-and-bit, huge and lightly-oiled, sweet-smelling. He pulled it out, and a hank of wire came with it, and leaping from the wire on to the floor, a small silver badge he hadn't seen before.

'What's that, Granda?'

'That's me honourable-discharge medal, that aah got after aah was gassed. Ye had to hev one o' those, or you got no peace in Blighty, if you weren't in uniform. Women giving ye the white feather, making out ye were a coward, not being at the Front. The military after ye, for being a deserter. Ye had to wear

17

that, an' carry yer discharge papers or ye didn't get a moment's peace, worse nor being at the Front, fightin' Jerry ... Put it back safe, there's a good lad ...' Granda's voice, vivid with memory for a moment, faded somewhere else again. Chas took the brace-and-bit, and fled.

Up to the corridor-cupboard by his bedroom. Soon the brace-and-bit were turning in his hands, tearing the pasted newspapers (in a boring bit, advocating Senna Pods for Constipation). Then came the curling shavings of yellow pine, smelling sweetly. After a long while, he felt the tip of the bit crunch through the last of the pine, and out into the open air behind the cupboard. He withdrew it, twisting the bit in reverse as Dad had once shown him, and put his eye to the hole.

He saw more corridor, just like the corridor he was standing in. Ending in a blank wall, ten yards away. A green, blistered door on the left, but no secret stair. No possible place the top of a secret stair could be. The green door was slightly ajar, inwards, but he could see nothing. The only window, in the right-hand wall, was thick with cobwebs; years of cobwebs. There was a little mat on the floor of the corridor, kicked up as if somebody had rushed past heedlessly and not bothered to replace it. Many, many years ago. The air in that corridor, the kicked mat, were the air and the mat of 1917. It was like opening a box full of 1917 ... more footsteps returning, a sigh, and then the bed-springs creaked again. Then came the sound of tuneless, doleful whistling, and a squeaking, like cloth polishing metal ...

Chas slammed the cupboard door and ran through the gathering gloom for the kitchen. He didn't realise

18

he still had Granda's brace-and-bit in his hands until he burst in on the family, gathered round the tea-table.

There were toasted teacakes for tea, dripping melted butter. And on the news, the announcer said the Navy had boarded and captured ten more German merchant-ships; they were being brought under escort into Allied ports. Slowly, Chas shook off the memory of the noises in the attic. Bedtime was far off yet. He dug into another teacake to console himself, and Nana loudly admired his appetite.

'Got a job for you after tea, our Chas. We've finished all the blackout curtains. When it's *really* dark, ye can go all round the outside o' the house, an' if ye spot a chink of light, ye can shout "Put that light out" just like a real air-raid warden.'

'That was no chink you saw in my bedroom last night,' said Holmes in a girlish simpering voice, 'that was an officer of the Imperial Japanese Navy . . .'

Mam didn't half give him a look, for talking smut in front of a child. Which was a laugh, because Chas had told Holmes that joke just an hour ago; he was working hard, softening Holmes up; know your enemy!

Chas was really enjoying himself, out there in the dark garden. He was again half-soaked, through walking into dripping bushes; he had trodden in something left behind by Miss Temple's dog, but such were the fortunes of war.

A little light glowed in the drawing-room window, where the blackout had sagged away from its frame.

He banged on the window sharply, indicating where the light-leak was, and inside, invisible, Nana's hand pressed the curtain into place. The little glow vanished.

'OK,' shouted Chas, 'that's all the ground floor.'

'Let me draw breath and climb upstairs,' Nana's voice came back faintly.

Chas paced back across the wet lawn; the grass squeaked under his wellies, and he practised making the squeaking louder. Then he glanced up at the towering bulk of The Elms. The blackouts on the first floor looked pretty good, though he wasn't going to let Nana get away with *anything*; it was a matter of National Security . . .

Reluctantly, his eyes flicked upwards . . . Granda's room was OK. There was no point in looking at the attics. There was only his own room, and there was no electric light in there, and his candle wasn't lit . . .

He looked up at the attics, and moaned.

The fifth window from the right was gently lit with candle-light. And there was the distinct outline of a man's head and shoulders, looking out of that window. He could only see the close-cropped hair, and the ears sticking out. But he knew the man was looking at him; he *felt* him looking, felt the caressing of his eyes. Then the man raised a hand and waved it in shy greeting. It was not the way Holmes would have waved a hand . . . or was Holmes taking the mickey out of him?

Suddenly, beside himself with rage, Chas shouted at the almost invisible face.

'Put that bloody light out! Put that bloody light out!'

He was still shouting hysterically when Nana came out and fetched him in.

'There's a face in that window next to mine!' shouted Chas. 'There *is*. Look!' He pointed a trembling finger.

But when he dared to look again himself, there was nothing but the faint reflection of drifting clouds, moving across the dim shine of the glass.

Nevertheless, when Nana picked him up bodily and carried him inside, as she often had when he was a little boy (she was a strong woman) Chas thought that she was trembling too.

He was given an extra drink, and set by the fire. 'Drink your tea as hot as you can,' said Nana. It was her remedy for all ills, from lumbago to Monday misery. Nana and Mam went on with the washing-up. They kept their voices low, but Chas still caught phrases: 'highly strung' and 'overactive brain'. Then Nana said, 'We'll move him down next to his Granda afore tomorrow night.' When Mam objected, Nana said sharply, 'Don't you *remember*? It was in all the papers. 'Course you'd only be a young lass at the time . . .' The whispering went on, but now they had lowered their voices so much, Chas couldn't hear a thing.

He wakened again in the dark. The luminous hands on his Mickey Mouse clock only said two o'clock. That meant he'd wakened up four times in four hours. It had never happened to him in his life before. He listened. Horrible bloody total silence; not even the wind sighing in the wireless aerial. Then, glad as a beacon on a headland to a lost ship, came the racking sound of Granda's cough downstairs.

It gave Chas courage; enough courage to put his ear to the wall of the room next door. And again he heard it; the creak of bedsprings, the endless tuneless whistling. Did he never bloody stop? Granda's cough again. Then bloody whistle, whistle, whistle. Fury seized Chas. He hammered on the wall with his fist, like Dad at home when the neighbours played the wireless too loud.

Then he wished he hadn't. Because the wall did not sound solid brick like most walls. It trembled like cardboard under his fist, and gave off a hollow sound. And at the same time, there was a noise of little things falling under his bed; little things like stones. He bent under the bed with his torch, without getting outside the bedclothes. A lump of the wall had cracked and fallen out. Plaster lay all over the bare floorboards, leaving exposed what looked like thin wooden slats. Perhaps there was a hole he could peep through . . . He put on his dressing-gown and crawled under the bed, and squinted at the place where the plaster had fallen off.

There seemed to be a thin glimmer of golden candle-light . . . Suddenly Chas knew there was no more sleep for him. He had a choice. The indignity of running down to Mam's room, like a baby with toothache. Or finding out just what the hell was going on behind that wall.

Downstairs, Granda coughed again.

Chas took hold of the first slat, and pulled it towards him. There was a sharp crack of dry wood, and the stick came out, pulling more plaster with it.

After that, he made a big hole, quite quickly. But the wall had *two* thin skins of slats and plaster. And the far one was still intact except for a long thin crack of golden light he couldn't see through. He'd just make a peephole, no bigger than a mousehole . . .

He waited again, for the support of Granda's cough, then he pushed the far slats.

Horror of horrors, they resisted stoutly for a moment, then gave way with a rush. The hole on the far side was as big as the hole this side. He could put his head and shoulders through it, if he dared. He just lay paralysed, listening. The man next door *must* have heard him; couldn't *not* have heard him.

Silence. Then a voice said,

'Come on in, if you're coming.' A Geordie voice, with a hint of a laugh in it. Not a voice to be afraid of.

He wriggled through, only embarrassed now, like Granda had caught him playing with his watch.

It was a soldier, sitting on a bed very like his own. A sergeant, for his tunic with three white stripes hung on a nail by his head. He was at ease, with his boots off and his braces dangling, polishing the badge of his peaked cap with a yellow duster. A tin of Brasso stood open on a wooden chair beside him; the sharp smell came clearly to Chas's nostrils. He was a ginger man with close-cropped ginger hair, the ends of which glinted in the candle-light. And a long sad ginger moustache. Chas thought he looked a bit old to be a soldier . . . or old-fashioned, somehow. Maybe that was because he was a sergeant.

'What you doing here?' he asked, then felt terribly rude. But the sergeant went on gently polishing his cap-badge.

'Aah'm on leave. From the Front.'

'Oh,' said Chas. 'I mean, what you doing *here*?'

'Aah knaa the girl downstairs. She knew aah needed a billet, so she fetched me up here.'

'Oh, Claire?'

The man didn't answer, merely went on polishing, whistling gently that same old tune.

'Do you stay up here all the time? Must be a bit boring, when you're on leave?'

The man sighed, and held his badge up to the candle, to see if it were polished enough. Then, still with his head on one side, he said mildly,

'You can do wi' a bit o' boredom, after what we've been through.'

'At the Front?'

'Aye, at the Front.'

'With the British Expeditionary Force?'

'Aye, wi' the British Expeditionary Force.'

'But the B.E.F.'s not done anything yet. The war's just started.'

'They'll tell you people on the home front anything. Aah've just started to realise that. Wey, we've marched up to Mons, and we fought the Germans at Mons, and beat 'em. Then we had to retreat from Mons, shelled all the way, and didn't even have time to bury our mates . . .'

'What's the worst thing? The German tanks?'

'Aah hevvn't seen no German tanks, though aah've seen a few of ours lately. No, the worst things is mud and rats and trench-foot.'

'What's trench-foot?'

The man beckoned him over, and took off his grey woollen sock. Up between his toes grew a blue mould

24

like the mould on cheese. The stink was appalling. Chas wrinkled his nose.

'It comes from standing all day in muddy water. First your boots gan rotten, then your feet. Aah'm lucky – they caught mine in time. Aah've know fellers lose a whole foot, wi' gangrene.' He put back his sock, and the smell stopped.

'Is that why you're up here, all day – 'cos you got trench-foot? You ought to be going out with girls – enjoying yourself. After all, you are home on leave . . . aren't you?'

The man turned and looked straight at him. His eyes . . . his eyes were sunk right back in his head. There were terrible, unmentionable things in those eyes. Then he said, 'Can yer keep a secret, Sunny Jim? Aah came home on leave, all right. That was my big mistake. Aah knew aah shuddn't. Aah didn't for three whole years . . . got a medal for my devotion to duty. Got made sergeant. Then they offered me a fortnight in Blighty, an' aah was tempted. The moment aah got home, an' saw the bonny-faced lasses, an' the green fields an' trees an' the rabbits playing, aah knew aah cud never gan back. So when me leave was up, the girl here, she's a bit sweet on me . . . she hid me up here. She feeds me what scraps she can . . .' He kicked an enamel plate on the floor, with a few crusts on it. 'Ye can get used to being in Hell, when you've forgotten there's owt else in the world, but when ye come home, an' realise that Heaven's still there . . . well, ye cannot bring yerself to go back to Hell.'

'You've got no guts,' said Chas angrily. 'You're a *deserter*.'

'Aye, aah'm a deserter all right. They'll probably

25

shoot me if they catch me ... but aah tell ye, aah had plenty of guts at the start. We used to be gamekeepers afore the war, Manny Craggs an' me. They found us very useful at the Front. We could creep out into No Man's Land wi'out making a sound, and bring back a brace of young Jerries, alive an' kicking an' ready for interrogation afore breakfast. It was good fun, at first. Till Manny copped it, on the Marne. It wes a bad time that, wi' the mud, an' Jerry so close we could hear him whispering in his own trench, and their big guns shelling our communication trench. We couldn't get Manny's body clear, so in the end we buried him respectful as we could, in the front wall o' our trench. Only the rain beat us. We got awake the next morning, an' the trench wall had part-collapsed, and there was his hand sticking out, only his hand. An' no way could we get the earth to cover it again. Can ye think what that was like, passing that hand twenty times a day? But every time the lads came past, they would shake hands wi' old Manny, an' wish him good morning like a gentleman. It kept you sane. Till the rats got to the hand; it was bare bone by the next morning, and gone the morning after. Aah didn't have much *guts* left after that ... but aah cudda hung on, till aah made the mistake o' coming on leave ... now aah'm stuck here, and there's neither forward nor backward for me ... just polishin' me brasses to look forward to. You won't shop me, mate? Promise?'

'Oh, it's nothing to do with me,' said Chas haughtily. The man was a coward, and nothing to be afraid of. He must have run away the moment he got to France; if he'd ever been to France at all ... the War had only been on three days. Making up these stupid stories to fool me 'cos he thinks I'm just an ignorant kid . . . 'I won't give you away.'

And with that, he wriggled back through the hole, and pushed his trunkful of toys against the hole in the wall, and went to bed and fast asleep. To show how much he despised a common deserter.

The following morning, when he wakened up, he was quite sure he'd dreamt the whole thing. Until he peeped under his bed and saw the trunk pushed against the wall, and plaster all over the floor. He pulled the trunk back, and shouted 'Hello' through the hole. There was no reply, or any other sound. Puzzled, he shoved his head through the hole. The room next door was empty. Except for the bed with its mattress, and the wooden chair lying on its side in a corner. Something made him look up to the ceiling above where the chair lay; there was a big rusty hook up there, driven into the main roofbeam. The hook fascinated him; he couldn't seem to take his eyes off it. You could hang big things from that, like sides of bacon. He didn't stay long, though; the room felt so very *sad*. Maybe it was just the dimness of the light from the cobwebbed windows. He wriggled back through the hole, pushed back the trunk to cover it, and cleaned up the fallen plaster into the chamber-pot and took it outside before Mam could spot it.

Anyway, the whole business was over; either the man had scarpered, or he'd dreamt the whole thing. People could walk in their sleep; why couldn't they knock holes in walls in their sleep too? He giggled at the thought. Just then, Mam came in, looking very brisk for business. He was to be moved downstairs immediately, next to Granda.

Suddenly, perversely, he didn't *want* to be moved. But Mam was adamant, almost hit him.

'What's the matter? What's got into you?'

But Mam, tight-lipped and pale-faced, just said, 'The very idea of putting you up here . . . get that map off the wall, quick!'

It was his war-map of Europe, with all the fronts marked with little Union Jacks and Swastikas and Hammer-and-Sickles. He began pulling the Union Jack pins out of the Belgian border with France. Then he paused. There, right in the middle of neutral Belgium, where no British soldier could possibly be, was the town of Mons. And there was a river called the Marne . . .

'Granda?'

The old, faded grey eyes turned from the window, from the scenes he would never talk about.

'Aye, son?'

'In the last war, was there a Battle of Mons?'

'Aye, and a Retreat from Mons, an' that was a bleddy sight worse. Shelled all the way, and no time to stop an' bury your mates . . .'

'And there was a Battle of the Marne . . . very rainy and muddy?'

'Aye. Never seen such mud till the Somme.'

Then Chas knew he'd been talking to a ghost. Oddly enough, he wasn't at all scared; instead, he was both excited and indignant. With hardly a moment's hesitation, he said, 'Thanks, Granda,' and turned and

28

left the room and walked up the stairs. Though he began to go faster and faster, in case his courage should run out before he got there. He wasn't sure about this courage he suddenly had; it wasn't the kind of courage you needed for a fight in the playground. It might leave him as suddenly as it had come. He pulled aside the trunk of toys, and went through the hole like a minor avalanche of plaster.

The sergeant was there, looking up from where he sat on the bed, still cleaning his cap-badge, like he'd been last night. The pair of them looked at each other.

'You're a ghost,' said Chas abruptly.

'Aah am *not*,' said the sergeant. 'Aah'm living flesh and blood. Though for how much longer, aah don't know, if aah have to go on sitting in this place, with nothing to do but polish this bloody cap-badge.'

His eyes strayed upwards, to the big rusty hook in the ceiling. Then flinched away, with a sour grimace of the mouth. 'Aah am flesh and blood, and that's a fact. Feel me.' And he held out a large hand, with little ginger hairs and freckles all over the back. His expression was so harmless and friendly, that after a long hesitation, Chas shook hands with him. The freckled hand indeed was warm, solid and human.

'I don't understand this,' said Chas, outraged. 'I don't understand this at *all*.'

'No more do aah,' said the sergeant. 'Aah'd ha' thought aah imagined you, if it hadn't been for that bloody great hole in the wall. Wi' your funny cap an' funny short trousers an' socks an' shoes. An' your not giving me away to the folks down below. Where are you from?'

'I think it's rather a case of *when* am I from,' said

29

Chas, wrinkling his brow. 'My date is the sixth of September 1939.'

'Aah *am* dreamin',' said the sergeant. 'Today's the sixth of September 1917. Unless aah'm out in me reckoning . . .' He nodded at the wall, where marks had been scrawled on the plaster with a stub of pencil. Six upright marks, each time, then a diagonal mark across them, making the whole group look like a gate or a fence. 'Eight weeks aah been in this hole . . .'

'Why don't you get out of it?'

'Aye,' said the sergeant. 'That'd be nice. Down into Shropshire, somewhere, where me old Da sent me to be a good gamekeeper. They'll be wantin' help wi' the harvest, now, wi' all the lads bein' away. Then lose meself into the green woods. Hole up in some cave in Wenlock Edge for winter, an' watch the rabbits an' foxes, and start to forget . . .' He screwed his eyes up tightly, as if shutting something out. 'That is, if God gave a man the power to forget. Aah don't need me sins forgiven; aah needs me memories forgiven.' He opened his blue eyes again. 'A nice dream, Sunny Jim, but it wouldn't work. Wi'out civvy clothes an' discharge papers, I wouldn't get as far as Newcastle . . .' Again, that glance up at the hook in the ceiling.

'I'll try and help,' said Chas.

'How?' The sergeant looked at him, nearly as trusting as a little kid.

'Well, look,' said Chas. He took off his school cap and gave it to the man. 'Put it on!'

The sergeant put it on with a laugh, and made himself go cross-eyed and put out his tongue. 'Thanks for the offer, but aah'd not get far in a bairn's cap . . .'

Chas snatched it back, satisfied. 'Wait and see.'

He had to wait a long time, before Nana was busy
hanging out the washing, and Mam holding the peg-
basket, and Granda was asleep. Then he moved in
quick, to the drawer where Granda kept his treasures.
The honourable-discharge badge and the discharge
papers were easy enough to find. Though he made a
noise shutting the drawer, Granda didn't waken. The
wardrobe door creaked too, but his luck held. He dug
deep into the smelly dark, full of the scents of Granda,
tobacco, Nana, fox-furs, dust and old age. He took
Granda's oldest overcoat, the tweed one he'd used
when he last worked as a stevedore, with the long oil-
stains and two buttons missing. And an oily old cap.
They would have to do. He pushed the wardrobe
door to, getting a glimpse of sleeping Granda in the
mirror. Then he was off, upstairs. He had a job getting
the overcoat through the hole. When he finally
managed it, he found the room was bare, cold and
empty. The chair was back in the corner, kicked away
from under the rusty iron hook. The sight filled him
with despair; the whole room filled him with despair.
But he laid the overcoat neatly on the bare mattress,
and the cap on top, and the badge, and the discharge
papers. Then, with a last look round, and a shudder
at the cold despair of the place, he wriggled out. At
least he had kept his word . . .

He haunted that room for a fortnight, more faith-
fully than any ghost. Perhaps *I* have become the ghost,
he thought, with a shudder. The coat and cap
remained exactly where they were. He tried to

imagine that the papers had moved a little, but he knew he was kidding himself.

Then came the night of the raid. The siren went at ten, while they were still eating their supper. Rather disbelievingly, they took cover in the cellars. Perhaps it was as well they did. The lone German bomber, faced with more searchlights and guns on the river than took its fancy, jettisoned its bombs on Preston. Three of the great houses fell in bitter ruin. A stick of incendiaries fell into the conservatory at The Elms, turning it into a stinking ruin of magnesium-smoke and frying green things.

Nana surveyed it in the dawn, and pronounced, 'That won't suit Tempy. And it's back home for you, my lad. This place is more dangerous than the bleddy docks, and yer Mam's still worrying about those bleddy tomato-plants . . .'

Chas packed, slowly and tiredly. Folded up his war-map of Europe. Thought he might as well get back Granda's badge and coat from upstairs.

But when he wriggled through, they weren't on the bed . . .

Who'd moved them, Nana or Mam? Why hadn't they *said* anything?

And the chair was upright by the empty bed, not kicked away in the corner. And on it, shining bright, something winked at Chas.

A soldier's cap-badge, as bright as if polished that very day. And on the plaster by the chair was scrawled a message, with a stub of pencil:

THANKS, LAD. THEY FIT A TREAT. SHAN'T WANT BADGE NO MORE — FAIR EXCHANGE NO ROBBERY, YOUR

GRANDFATHER'S A BRAVE MAN — KEPT RIGHT ON TO
THE END OF THE ROAD — MORE THAN I WILL DO, NOW.
RESPECTFULLY YOURS, 1001923 MELBOURNE, W. J., SGT.

Chas stood hugging himself, and the cap-badge,
with glee. He had played a trick on time itself . . .

But time, once interfered with, had a few tricks up
its sleeve too. The next few minutes were the weirdest
he'd ever known.

Brisk footsteps banged along the corridor. Stopped
outside his room next door, looked in, saw he wasn't
there, swept on . . .

Swept on straight through where the corridor-
cupboard was . . . or should be. The door of the soldier's room began to open. Chas could have screamed.
The door had no right to open. It was fastened away,
inaccessible behind the corridor-cupboard . . .

But there was no point in screaming, because it
was only Nana standing there, large as life. 'There you
are, you little monkey. Aah knew ye'd be here, when
aah saw that bleddy great hole in the wall . . . ye
shouldn't be in this room.'

'Why not?'

'Because a poor feller hanged himself in this room
— a soldier who couldn't face the trenches. Hanged
himself from that very hook in the ceiling, standing
on this very chair . . .' She looked up; Chas looked up.

There was no longer any hook in the beam. There
had been one, but it had been neatly sawn off with a
hacksaw. Years ago, because the sawn edge was red
with rust.

33

Nana passed a hand over her pale weary face. 'At least ... Aah *think* aah heard that poor feller hanged himself ... they blocked off this room wi' a broom-cupboard.'

She peered round the door, puzzled. So did Chas. There was no broom-cupboard now. Nor any mark where a broom-cupboard might have been. The corridor ran sheer and uninterrupted, from one end to the other.

'Eeh,' said Nana, 'your memory plays you some funny tricks when you get to my age. Aah could ha sworn ... Anyway, what's Melly going to say when aah tell her ye made a bleddy great hole in her wall? Aah expect you want me to blame it on Hitler and the Jarmans?'

'Who's Melly? You mean Tempy?' said Chas, grasping at straws in his enormous confusion.

'What d'you mean, who's Melly? Only Mrs Melbourne who owns this house, and runs the school, and has given ye more ten-bob notes than aah care to remember.'

Chas wrinkled up his face. Was it Miss Temple, shoes, legs and gown, who gave him ten-bob notes ... or was it Mrs Melbourne, who sat kindly in a chair and smiled at him? Who, when he was smaller, had sometimes taken him down to the kitchen for a dish of jelly and ice-cream from her wonderful new-fangled refrigerator? He had a funny idea they were one and the same person, only different. Then time itself, with a whisk of its tail, whipped all memory of Miss Temple from his mind; and his mind was the last place on earth in which Miss Temple had ever existed.

'Aah don't know what the hell you made that hole

in the wall for,' said Nana. 'You could just as easily have walked in through the door; it's never been locked.'

Chas could no longer remember himself, as he tucked the shining cap-badge in his pocket, and gave Nana a hand to take his belongings down to the taxi.

'Why did aah think a feller hanged himself in that room?' muttered Nana. 'Must be getting morbid in me old age . . .'

'Yeah,' said Chas, squinting at the cap-badge surreptitiously.

Almost a Ghost Story

'Is the abbey really haunted?' asked Rachel.

'Well, there's the ghost of the nun,' teased Mum.

'Rubbish,' said Dad, without taking his eyes off the road. 'What would a nun be doing in a *monastery*?'

'There's the Nun's Grave,' said Mum, leading him on. And getting him on his high horse, like she always could.

'It's been proved, time and again, that the Nun's Grave's an eighteenth-century folly. Bits of the old church dug up and stuck together to improve the view from the squire's drawing-room windows. They've excavated it three times – nothing but black-beetles.' He changed gear grumpily. The long driveway to the abbey had become very bumpy. The headlights turned it into a series of miniature mountains and black caverns.

A tall grey shape with upstretched arms glowed dimly into view, far away; grew and grew till every last twig glistened white against the darkness; then, when it seemed about to engulf them, whirled away overhead. Then another, and another. Once, said Dad, there'd been a whole avenue of beech-trees, but each winter gale left fresh gaps. Huge beech-corpses lay at intervals, shorn of their branches by power-saws.

'All the same,' said Mum, 'it feels funny, coming back after all this time. How long has it stood empty?'

'Twenty years – since the country-club closed. I was there when it happened – we were under drinking-age, but they were letting in anybody with money at the end. Anyway, the barman dropped a crate of beer in the upstairs bar, and the beer trickled through the floorboards and blew all the wiring. You ought to have seen the sparks. We thought we were all going up in a blue light – we never stopped running till we reached Davenham. Club closed straight after . . .' Dad laughed to himself, at the memory of being a young rip; he was never cross for long. But Mum couldn't leave him alone.

'Perhaps the nun disapproved of all that boozing . . .'

'*Rubbish*! That electric wiring must've come out of the ark. It's just that they tried to turn the abbey into so many things – Civil Defence Centre, school for accountants – none of them prospered.'

His voice trailed off. The gaunt beeches continued to appear and whirl overhead. Rachel snuggled up tight behind Mum and Dad's shoulders. It was suddenly cold, dark and lonely in the back of the Maxi. There was a draught and a rattle from the right-hand door.

'Daddy, my door's not shut properly . . .'

Dad reached behind him without stopping, opened the door and slammed it solidly. That made Rachel feel better. So did the string of car-lights in front; the distant headlights behind, bouncing wildly into the sky as the following cars hit the cart-ruts in the drive. Rachel was glad they weren't alone.

'It's a good place for a Christmas concert,' said Mum, snuggling down into her fur collar with an enjoyable shiver. 'With a ghost an' all . . .'

'The new owners are desperate for funds. Place is full of dry-rot. They say that upstairs the hardboard partitions are buckled with it, like a shell had hit them. And down in the cellars, it grows out of the walls like an old man's beard.'

'D'you think it'll be safe?' asked Mum, suddenly really worried.

'*You* bought the tickets. *You* wanted the thrill!'

'I don't want to break me ankle.'

'That's more likely than any flippin' ghost.'

'Were the monks good men?' asked Rachel, suddenly.

'Bunch of layabouts,' Dad snorted. 'Lived a life of idle luxury. Tried to build a church bigger'n Westminster Abbey – for only twenty of them. Only the walls blew down in a great storm, afore they got the roof on, an' that was that. But they still went on squeezing their tenants for every penny they had. Tenants murdered one monk, an' played football wi' his head.'

'Oh,' said Rachel.

'That nun,' said Mum dreamily. 'The book said she fell in love with the wicked Abbot an' pined away.'

'That book was the worst Victorian novel ever written. Ever tried reading it?'

'Only the first five pages. Then I skipped, looking for juicy bits.'

'Find any?'

Mum shook her head as they swung on to the rough grassy car-park.

'Looks funny, all lit up,' said Dad. 'I came past it

38

many a time, in me courting days, an' never a light but the moon glinting on the windows.'

'You never brought me,' said Mum.

'Where's the Nun's Grave?' asked Rachel.

'I'll show you,' said Dad, glancing at his watch and getting his big rubber torch out of the glove compartment. 'We've got five minutes before it starts.'

'Not me,' shivered Mum. 'Give me the tickets and I'll keep your seats.'

Dad and Rachel walked down the great dark side of the abbey; the grass was so frosty it scrunched under their feet.

'Them's the Abbot's chimneys,' said Dad, nodding upwards. Rachel stared up at the great black hexagons, towering above the roofline.

'How long have the abbots been gone?'

'Henry the Eighth got shot of them – sold the house to the Holcrofts. It passed from hand to hand after that – nobody kept it long. Last real owner went to farm in Kenya in 1940. Then it was a prisoner-of-war camp – Jerries. Anyway, here's your so-called *grave*.'

He shone the torch. There was a hexagonal stone base, then a square pillar, than a little stone house on top, with a figure sitting in the arch. In the torchlight, Rachel could see that the figure's hands and face had been worn away by wind and rain. And yet, as Dad flicked the torch contemptuously around, you could almost make out a little face ... nose and eyes ... but they changed, as the light flickered.

'She's got a headdress like a nun!'

'All ladies wore them, in those days. C'mon, or your Mum'll be having a fit.'

There was a man on the door, in overcoat, hat and

muffler up to his ears. He waved them through, with a mumble through the muffler, because Mum had explained about the tickets. They were in a long, long vaulted corridor, colder than outside. It had been painted a filthy bright orange by the owners of the country-club, but that made it more spooky, not less. Like Dracula wearing make-up.

'There's the Ladies, in case you need it,' said Dad. They walked on and on, under the orange vaults and weak buzzing neons, past the black, black windows.

'This was the monks' cloister,' said Dad.

They finally came to another man in coat, hat and muffler, at the foot of the grand staircase. There was a wooden gargoyle sitting on the newelpost, half-lion, half-dragon. It watched Rachel with sly dark carved eyes as if waiting for a chance to bite her. There was a faint hum of human voices, trickling down the staircase-well.

From the safety of the stairs, Rachel looked back, trying to see the sign for the Ladies. The far end of the cloister seemed lost in a thin black mist, as if somebody had left a window open, and let the dark in.

The great hall was full; a sea of fur coats, fur hats, suede boots. Nobody was taking anything off, for small draughts curled round your legs like icy snakes, every time a latecomer opened the hall doors. They found Mum nicely placed by a huge fireplace that looked like a Gothic tombstone, complete with a pair of winged figures that certainly weren't angels. It was extravagantly filled with a roaring log fire. Some of the logs were three feet long.

'Central heating's not much cop,' said Mum. 'I'm

roasting one side and freezing the other. Let's cuddle up, George. Put Rachel in the middle.'

They'd no sooner settled than a tall thin grey-haired man rose to his feet across the sea of fur hats. People eventually stopped losing and finding their gloves, talking, and waving to friends, and settled to listen. As the gentleman had floppy hair and a great sheaf of papers, and had to keep pushing his hair out of his eyes and retrieving papers from the floor, he was not easy to listen to. But it appeared he was the secretary of the charity that had bought the abbey. They hoped to turn it into a children's home. They had saved the abbey from the very brink of disaster; pulled eight-foot ash trees out of cracks in its walls; spent all one stormy night on the roof, holding down the slates with their outspread bodies.

'Otherwise you wouldn't be sitting here tonight . . .'

A lot of fur hats tilted, as people looked nervously at the ceiling. It certainly carried a lot of peculiar spreading stains, like maps of South America and Norway.

'I think we can guarantee your safety this evening,' said the secretary, and dropped his notes again. There was an anxious titter, thin as the blowing of dead leaves on an autumn night.

He told them of the charity's first night in the abbey, with ninety-one locked rooms and only ninety keys. How all the lights failed half an hour after dusk; how his bedroom was nearly a hundred yards from the kitchen.

'But we learnt that night that there are either no ghosts in the abbey, or, if there are, they are friendly to our cause, and want the abbey to survive. So I

41

think they would be pleased to see us all gathered here tonight, a week before Christmas, so that the old house is alive again . . .'

Then the musicians walked in. Three plump young men in crumpled dinner-jackets, with dark crinkly hair and horn-rimmed spectacles. They might have been brothers. And a very elegant lady with long neck and long graceful bare arms, who was going to play the cello. They announced themselves as the Rococo Ensemble, and began plucking and tweaking nervously at their violins and double-bass. The swan-necked lady became visibly aware of the temperature in the hall and the writhing icy snakes from the doors, which kept opening and shutting in the draught, as if someone kept meaning to come in, then changed their mind. Rachel watched the lady's arms and neck turn first purple and then blue, in interesting patches; saw the lady look longingly at the thick woolly stole at her feet, then decide that one could not really play the cello wearing a stole . . .

Then their leader announced they would begin with one of Vivaldi's 'Four Seasons' and they had decided to make it . . . Winter . . .

More thin laughter. Then the four musicians looked at each other with raised eyebrows and cold little smiles, and were off.

And it was very fine; but very wintry. Rachel's eyes swept the ceiling in a dream. Huge oak beams soared to the top of the roof . . . 'the wicked Abbot's original beams,' said Dad in a whisper. In between, later families had plastered their coats-of-arms, boasting who'd married whom. But Rachel wasn't much bothered by who'd married whom. She had not liked that phrase

42

about the old house coming back to life. Her mind roamed round the house. The ancient central-heating system, passing through wall after wall, from darkened room to darkened room, hissing hot water and steam and totally failing to keep the cold at bay. The black attics, where the partitions were buckled as if a shell had hit them. The long orange cloister that led to the loo, full of smoky dark at the far end; the cellars where the dry-rot grew out of the walls like an old man's beard . . .

And all the time Vivaldi's music of raindrops pattered on their ears, and the air grew colder. Only the ceiling looked warm, lit with a rich yellow light, from concealed spotlights hidden behind the beams.

The music ended; the musicians almost ran for the comfort of their changing-room and its two-bar electric fire. The secretary announced that the buffet was now open in the state dining-room, with a choice of wine or hot coffee. There was nearly a stampede, scarcely checked by middle-class decorum.

The state dining-room was fabulous. A huge white marble fireplace with columns, a huge white door with columns, and a white-and-gilt plaster ceiling. Pity there was a gaping black hole in the ceiling, with a raw new wooden post thrust up through it, high as a fir tree. The secretary announced that it was dry rot, but perfectly well in hand. Somebody had pinned a blue notice to the post, saying 'Queue here for coffee'.

The state dining-table was smothered in mini pork pies, chicken croquettes and huge cream gâteaus from end to end.

'Good spread,' said Dad, handing yellow paper plates around.

'The plates are very small,' said Mum. 'That won't hold much!'

'You can come round again.'

'What, after this bunch of vultures have been through it? Anyway, those sausage-rolls have been kept warm too long – they're all shrivelled.'

'That table's a lovely bit of mahogany.'

'You can't eat mahogany!'

Rachel went round again three times, and had two cups of very hot coffee. Then the standing-up and the cold and the two cups of coffee began to make their effects felt. She knew she ought to go to the loo.

Then she thought about the misty orange cloister . . .

'Mum – do you want the loo? I know where it is.'

'Shhh – in public – certainly not. These vol-au-vents aren't bad, George. Try one.'

Rachel desperately kept her legs pressed together. Once they sat down again she'd be all right.

'Will you please take your seats again, ladies and gentlemen.'

'Mum – I've got to go . . .'

'Come on, then. Hurry up – it's starting. Trust *you* . . .'

'Come with me?'

'Certainly not. You're a big girl now – nearly twelve.'

There was no choice. Rachel went. Running down the Grand Staircase she met a few people coming up, stamping out their cigarettes on the stone, then picking up the flattened dog-ends guiltily and putting them in their breast-pockets. Still, there was still the man

44

on the door, at the far end of the cloister . . . he'd be sort of company.

She met him hurrying up the stairs too, blowing on his hands and very glad to leave his lonely post. She was now quite alone.

She began walking along the cloister, towards the mist of dark. She couldn't bear to look at it. She walked on, counting the cracks between the paving-stones instead. But she had to look up, eventually.

There was a black-robed figure, standing right outside the entrance to the Ladies. Black from head to foot, and its back turned towards her. Absolutely still.

Terror transfixed Rachel. Then the figure moved slightly, and the black robe lifted a little from the floor, to reveal a pair of sparkling diamante heels.

Blood surged back into Rachel's heart in great painful pumps. No nun ever wore diamante heels. The figure turned, to reveal a plump lady in black velvet evening-cloak and sequinned dress, with a kind face and dangly earrings. She gave a start when she saw Rachel, then smiled.

'Oh, you did make me jump! Isn't this a funny old place? Which way is it back? I'm quite lost.'

'If you wait for me a tick,' said Rachel desperately, 'I'll show you.'

The woman smiled understandingly.

Rachel had never been so quick in her life.

Things really began to go wrong in the second half. The musicians tried over and over again to get their instruments tuned properly, and couldn't seem to manage it.

'It's the cold,' said Dad. 'It affects the cat-gut.'

'It's affecting my guts,' said Mum. 'I wish now I'd gone with our Rachel.'

More in desperation than hope, the musicians launched off into some Albinoni, with a half-hearted little quip about hot rhythms. Albinoni would not have liked it. The two violins could not get together, and wowled frequently and horribly. The swan-necked lady had donned not only her stole, but also a clashing polo-neck sweater, and it showed in her playing. The double-bass, stout backstop, seemed somehow to get detached; its sound seemed to be coming from one corner of the rafters.

'Funny acoustics,' whispered Dad. 'Must be a layer of warm air up there.'

'You must be joking,' said Mum. 'I've just lost my last layer of warm air, and I won't tell you where from. There's no *heat* in this fire.'

Rachel held forward her hand, and it was true. The fire roared up the chimney as fiercely as ever, but not a trace of heat could she feel. All, musicians and audience, seemed locked in some terrible refrigerator.

And then, up among the rafters and the ceiling spot-lights, Rachel saw a little black dancing shadow, moving up and down erratically, like a flake of soot from a burning chimney; like a little black butterfly.

She watched it uneasily for a bit, then tugged Dad's sleeve.

'Moth,' said Dad. 'Been hibernating. Been wakened up by the heat of the spotlights.'

'What heat?' asked Mum, from the depths of her collar.

Rachel forgot the music, went on watching the

46

moth. There was a funny effect. As it fluttered nearer the spotlights, seeking light and warmth, the spotlights threw its shadow on the ceiling, magnified many times. The shadow looked as big as a bird, waxing and waning, depending where the moth flew.

And then it seemed that the moth itself, the solid black shape, became as big as its shadow, and the shadow grew many times bigger. Big as a person.

People began to notice. Little indrawn breaths came from the women; then little shrieks as the thing came lower, with wavering uncertain flight. The music flew wilder and wilder, as even the musicians turned their heads to follow its flight, without stopping playing.

Suddenly it was hovering right in front of Rachel's face. Black, black like a robe, with a little bit of white and paleness on top.

She stared and stared and stared . . .

Then Dad's arm crashed across, with his open tweed cap in his fist. It hit the black thing a terrible sideways blow, and flung it into the heart of the roaring flames in the great Gothic fireplace. There it hovered a moment, still fluttering to live. Then there was a puff of dark grey smoke, and a slight and evil smell, and it was quite gone.

'Bloody bat,' said Dad, uncomfortably, as everyone turned to stare at him. 'Nasty bloody things. Good riddance to bad rubbish.'

Then Rachel was crying uncontrollably. Dad tried shaking her; Mum tried cuddling her. But it was no good.

Guiltily they led her towards the doors that still

opened and closed a little in the draught, as if someone was trying to get in and failing.

The tall grey man tried to apologise. 'Nests in the chimneys . . . nearly smoked us out this morning . . . early days.'

But no one could hear him, because Rachel would not stop crying.

Audience and musicians watched them go, sympathetically.

At the door, Rachel broke away, back into the room.

'But didn't you *see*,' she shouted. 'It had a human face! It wanted me to help her. Didn't you *see*?'

The doors closed behind her, as Mum and Dad dragged her out.

'Poor child – quite overwrought.'

'She's had a nasty fright – very nasty.'

'They're very imaginative at that age . . .'

The Albinoni picked up wearily, like a record-player switched on when a record has been left half-played. The audience settled back into its fur coats and suede boots, to weather out the concert.

But there was never another concert in that abbey.

The Vacancy

It was in a side-street, in the window of a little brown-brick office. Neatly written, on fresh clean card:

'Vacancy available.

For a bright keen lad.'

Martin pulled up, surveyed it suspiciously. Why specify a lad? Illegal, under the Sex-discrimination Act. England was a land of equal opportunity; to be unemployed. Martin laughed, without mirth. The employment police would be on to that straight away, and he didn't want to get involved with the employment police. But perhaps the employment police wouldn't bother coming down here. It was such a dingy lost little street. In all his travels he'd never come across a street so lost.

He parked his bike against the dull brown wall. An early 1980s racing-bike, his pride and joy. Salvaged from the conveyor-belt to the metal-eater in the nick of time, rusty and wheelless. He'd haunted the metal-eater for months after that, watching for spare-parts. The security cameras round the metal-eater watched him; or *seemed* to watch him. They moved constantly, but you could never tell if they were on automatic.

Anyway, he'd rebuilt the bike; resprayed it. Spent three months' unemployment benefit on oil and aero-

49

sols. Now it shone, and got him round from district to district. The district gate-police didn't like him wheeling it through, but it wasn't illegal. The government hadn't bothered making bikes illegal, just stopped production altogether, including spare-parts. Cycling had imperceptibly died out.

You had to be careful, travelling from district to district. In some, the unemployed threw stones and worse. In others, it was said, they strung up strangers from lamp-posts, as government spies. Though that was probably a rumour spread by the gate-police. He'd never suffered more than the odd, half-hearted stone, even in the beginning. Now, they all knew his bike, gathered round to get the news.

But he'd travelled far that morning, further than ever before, because of the row with his father.

'Your constant moaning makes me sick,' the old man had said, putting on his worker's cap with the numbered brass badge. 'I keep you – you get free sport, free contraceptives, free drugs and a twenty-channel telly. You lie in bed till tea-time. At your age . . .'

'You had a job,' shouted Martin. 'In 1981, at the age of sixteen you were given a job, which you still have.'

'Some job. Two hours a day. Four times in two hours a bloody bell rings and I check a load of dials and write the numbers in a book that nobody needs and nobody reads. Call that a job for a trained electrician?'

'You have a reason to get up in the morning – mates at work.'

'*Mates*? I see the fore-shift when I clock on, and

50

the back-shift when I clock off. My nearest *mate* is ten minutes' walk away. Where *you* going?'

'Out. On my bike.'

'You think you're so bloody clever wi' that bike. *And* your bloody wanderings. Why can't you stay where you were born, like everybody else?'

''Cos I'm not like everybody else. And *they're* not going to make me.'

'You want to button your lip, talking like that. Or *they'll* hear you.'

'Or *you'll* tell them.' Then Martin saw the look on his father's face and was sorry. The old man would never do a thing like that. Not like some fathers ...

He was still staring at the card offering the vacancy when a blond kid came out, and spat on the pavement with a lot of feeling.

'Been havin' a go?' asked Martin mildly.

'It's a con,' said the kid. 'They set you an intelligence-test that would sink the Prime Minister.' He was no slouch or lout, either. Still held himself upright; switched-on blue eyes. Another lost sixth-former. 'Waste of time!'

'I don't know ...' said Martin. In school, he'd been rather sharp on intelligence-tests.

'Suit yourself,' said the blond kid, and walked away.

Martin still hesitated. Then it started to rain, spattering his thin jeans. That settled it. The grey afternoon looked so pointless that even failing an intelligence-test sounded a big thrill. Sometimes they gave you coffee ...

He walked in; the woman sitting knitting looked

51

up, bored, plump and ginger. Pale blue eyes swam behind her spectacles like timid tropical fish.

'What's the vacancy?'

'Oh . . . just a general vacancy. Want to apply?'

He shrugged. 'Why not?' She passed him a ballpoint and a many-paged green intelligence-test.

'Ready?' She clicked a stopwatch into action, and put it on the desk in front of her, as if she'd done it a million times before. 'Forty minutes.' He sighed with satisfaction as his ballpoint sliced into the test. It was like biting a ham sandwich, like coming home.

An hour later, she was pushing back agitated wisps of ginger hair and speaking into the office intercom, her voice a squeak of excitement, a near-mad glint in her blue tropical fish eyes.

'Mr Boston – I've just tested a young man – a very high score – a very high score indeed. Highest score in *months*.'

'Contain yourself, Miss Feather. What is the score?' It was a deliberately dull voice that not only killed her excitement dead as a falling pigeon, but made her pull down her plaid skirt, already well below her knees.

'Four hundred and ninety-eight, Mr Boston.'

'Might be worth giving him a PA 52. Yes, try him with a PA 52. We've nothing better to do this afternoon.'

PA 52 was twice as thick as the other one. As Martin took it, a little warm shiver trickled down his spine. Gratitude? To *them*? For what? Not rejecting him outright, like the blond kid? He smashed down the gratitude with a heavy mental fist; they'd only fail him further on. They were just playing with him. They had no job; there were no jobs. Still, he might as well get something out of his moment of triumph.

'Could I have a cup of coffee? Before I start?'

'Oh, I think we could manage a cup of coffee. You start, and I'll put it by your elbow when it's ready.' She clucked around him like she was an old mother-hen, and he the only egg she'd ever laid. Smoothly, with a sense of ascending power, he began to cut through PA 52.

'Sit down,' said Mr Boston, steepling long nicotined fingers. He consulted PA 52 slyly, slantingly. 'Erm . . . Martin, isn't it?'

'Mmmm,' said Martin. He thought that Boston, with his near-religious air of relaxed guilt and pin-stripe brown suit (shiny at cuff and elbow, and no doubt backside, if backside had been visible) was more like a careers-officer than any employer. Employers were much better dressed, ran frantic fingers through their hair, and expected to answer the phone any minute. Still, he'd only met two employers in his life; they'd turned him down before he left school.

'I see you're interested in working with people?'

'Oh, yes, *very*,' said Martin, outwardly eager, inwardly mocking. You were taught in first-year always to say you were terribly keen on people. Jobs with machinery no longer existed; only computers talked to computers now.

'I see leadership-potential here.' Boston peered

into PA 52 like it was a crystal-ball. 'A lot of leadership. Do you find it easy to persuade others ... your friends ... to do what *you* want?'

'Oh yes.' Martin thought of the copies of his underground-newspaper, rolled up and pushed down the hollow tubes of his bike, ready for distribution to the various districts. Getting the newspaper-team together had taken a lot of persuasion. Persuading pretty little girls to be the news-gatherers, which meant sleeping with grubby elderly civil servants for the sake of their pillowtalk. Getting the printers, with their old hand-operated cyclostyling machine, set up in a makeshift hut in the middle of Rubbishtip 379, after the spy-cameras, sprayed daily with saltwater, had rusted solid and stood helpless as stuffed birds. 'Yes, I find it easy to persuade others to do what I want.'

'*Good*,' said Mr Boston. He leaned forward to his intercom. 'Miss Feather – bring our friend Martin here another cup of coffee – the continental blend this time, I think.' Somewhere in the small terraced building, a large electrical machine began to hum, slightly but not unpleasantly vibrating the old walls. Some percolator, Martin thought, with a slight smile. He was already starting to feel proprietorial, patronising about this old dump.

Boston re-steepled his fingers, and slantingly consulted PA 52 again. 'And bags of initiative ... you're a good long way from home, here. Five whole districts. Have you walked? You must be fit.'

'I've got an old bicycle ...'

'A bike? Bless my soul.' So great was Boston's surprise that he took off his spectacles, folded their arms neatly across each other, and popped them into the breast-pocket of his suit. He surveyed Martin with naked eyes, candid, weary and brown-edged as an old dog's. 'I haven't seen a bike in years, though I did my share of riding as a boy. Where did you find this bike?'

'At the metal-eater. Had to build it up from bits.'

Mr Boston's excitement was now so great that he had to put his spectacles on again. 'Yes, yes, your mechanical aptitude and manual dexterity show up here on PA 52. And your patience. But . . .' and his voice fell like the Tellypreacher's when he came to the Sins of the Flesh, 'it wasn't awfully honest, was it, taking that bike away from the metal-eater? It already belonged to the State . . .'

Martin's heart sank. This was the point where the job-interview fell apart. Even before he got his second cup of coffee. It had been going so well . . . but he knew better than to try to paper over the cracks. He hardened his heart and got up.

'Stuff the State,' he said, watching Boston's eyes for the expression of shock that would be the last pay-off of this whole lousy business.

But Boston didn't look shocked. He took off his spectacles and waved them; a look of boyish glee suffused his face.

'Stuff the state . . . exactly. Well, not exactly . . .' he corrected himself with an effort. 'We all depend upon the State, but we know it isn't omniscient. To the mender of washing-machines, the State supplies split-pins at a reasonable price, within a reasonable time. But suppose our supply of split-pins has run out already, because we imprudently neglected to re-order in time? We still want our split-pins *now* – even if we

55

have to pay twice the legal price. That is my . . . our . . . little business. Greasing the wheels of state, as I always tell my wife (who is a director of our little firm).' He polished his spectacles enthusiastically with a little stained brown cloth, taken from his spectacle-case for the purpose.

'And if we get caught?' asked Martin; but his mood soared.

'A heavy fine . . . the firm will pay. Or a short prison-sentence; that soon passes. We're commercial criminals, not political. We do not wish to overthrow the State, only oil its wheels, oil its wheels. The State understands this.'

They eyed each other. Martin still thought Boston didn't talk like a businessman. But the chances this firm offered . . . His own bedsitter, perhaps a firm's van . . . better still, a chance to smuggle on his own behalf. Not just paper for the newspaper . . . perhaps high-grade steel tubing for guns. He looked at Boston doubtfully; jobs just didn't grow on trees like this. Boston licked his lips, almost pleading, like an old spaniel.

'Sounds a good doss,' said Martin doubtfully.

'Then you accept the vacancy? You're a most suitable candidate.'

Miss Feather came in with the second cup of coffee.

'Will there be a chance to travel?' asked Martin.

'Almost immediately,' said Mr Boston, and Miss Feather nodded in smiling agreement. 'We will have to process you now. Would you mind waiting in here?'

The waiting-room was tiny. Just enough room for a bentwood chair, and a toffee-varnished rack containing a few worn copies of the State magazine at the very end of their life. Martin was surprised any-body had ever bothered to read them; everyone knew they were all glossy lies. There was a strange selection of posters on the walls – Fight Tooth Decay, an advert for the local museum of industrial sewing-machines, and a travel poster featuring an unknown tropical island. Martin wondered if his new job would take him anywhere near there. His head was whirling with the strange drunkenness of accepting and being accepted. Blood pounded all over his body. The vibrations of that damned machine were coming through the waiting-room walls, and going right through his head. It sounded a clapped-out machine, as if it was trying but would never make it.

Too late, the tiny size of the waiting-room warned him; the oppressive warmth. He pulled at the closed door, but it had no handle this side. He hammered on it; heavy metal.

Then there was a crack of blue darkness inside his head. When he opened his eyes again, he was standing in a room exactly the same size, but walled with stain-less steel and excruciatingly cold. He shivered, but not just with cold.

There was a great round window set in the door. In the window floated the moon, only it was too big, pale blue and green, scarfed in a white that could only be clouds. Below were low white hills like ash-tips. Nearer, lying on the ashy soil, what looked like heaps of the stringy frozen chops you found in the deep-freeze of the most wretched supermarkets. From among the heaps, white skulls watched him, patiently waiting.

But much worse was the black sky, the totally black

sky. In which stars glowed huge and incandescent, red, blue, yellow, orange. Some pulsed, at varying rhythms; others shone steadily.

'There!' Boston's voice came from a grille above the door, crackly with radio-static. 'There's your vacancy, Martin. Outer space. The biggest vacancy there is!' His voice was almost gentle, almost proud, almost pleading. 'Look your fill – I can only give you another minute.'

Quite unable to think of anything else to do, Martin continued to gaze at the pulsing stars. Then the door of the capsule slid aside. His body, sucked outwards by the vacuum, turning slowly in the low gravity, exploded in half-a-dozen places in rapid succession. The force of the explosions shot out great clouds of red vapour, that sank swiftly to the surface of the white ash. Continuing explosions drove his disintegrating body across the mounds of his predecessors like an erratic fire-cracker. Then, indistinguishable from the rest of the heaps, except for its fresh redness, it settled to the freeze-drying, vacuum-drying of total vacancy.

'It always seems to me a pity,' said Mr Boston, 'that anything as wonderful as the Moon Teleport should have been reduced to *this* use. We could have conquered space, if we'd only discovered how to bring people *back*. Now it's no more than a garbage-disposal unit.'

'I always feel so flat afterwards,' said Miss Feather. She lifted a faded print of Constable's *Haywain* from the wall, revealing a row of stainless-steel buttons and a digital read-out in green.

11,075,019

She tapped the buttons rapidly. The number went down one.

11,075,018

Then resumed its inexorable climb.

11,075,019
11,075,021

Miss Feather gave a slight shudder of distaste, and replaced *The Haywain*.

'Pity we can't send them all that way.' She pressed her hairstyle back into place with the aid of her compact-mirror.

'Do you know how much it costs to send *one* to the moon?' asked Boston. 'No, we can only send the dangerous ones. The ones that qualify for the vacancy.'

'*Was* he dangerous?'

'He might have become so. Intelligence, leadership, initiative, mobility, ingenuity, curiosity – all the warning signs were there. It doesn't pay to be sentimental, Miss Feather – I believe young tiger-cubs are quite cuddleable in their first weeks of life. Nevertheless, they become tigers. We remove the tiger-cubs so that the rest, the sheep, may safely graze, as one might put it. I only fear we might not catch enough tiger-cubs in time. The young keep on coming like an inexorable flood, wanting what their fathers and grandfathers had. They could sweep us away.'

They sat looking at each other, in mildly depressed silence.

'That bicycle was a sure sign,' said Boston at last. 'Most original – first I've seen in years. Originality is always a danger. I'd better get the bike off the street, before it's noticed. Ring the metal-eater people, will you?'

Miss Feather rang; put the kettle on for another cup of coffee. Mr Boston came back empty-handed, perturbed.

'It's gone. Someone's taken it.'

'A sneak-thief?'

'Then he's a very stupid sneak-thief,' said Boston savagely. 'Stealing a unique object he'd never dare ride in public.'

'You don't think one of his friends . . . should we ring for the police?' Her hand went to the necklace round her throat, nervously.

'To report the theft of a bicycle that didn't belong to us in the first place? They'd think that pretty irregular. They'd want to know where our young friend Martin had got to . . .'

'Shall we ring the Ministry?'

'My dear Miss Feather, they'd think we were losing our nerve. You don't fancy premature retirement, do you?'

She paled. He nodded, satisfied. 'Then I think we'd better just sit it out.'

Facing each other with a growing silent unease, as the light faded in the grubby street outside, they settled down to wait.

The Night Out

ME and Carpet were just finishing a game of pool, working out how to pinch another game before the kids who'd booked next, when Maniac comes across.

Maniac was playing at Hell's Angels again. Home-made swastikas all over his leathers and beer-mats sewn all over his jeans. Maniac plays at everything, even biking. Don't know how we put up with him, but he hangs on. Bike Club's a tolerant lot.

'Geronimo says do you want to go camping tonight?' chirps Maniac.

'Pull the other one,' says Carpet. 'Cos the last we seen of Geronimo, he was pinching forks and spoons out of the Club canteen to stuff up Maniac's exhaust. So that when Maniac revved up, he'd think his big-end had gone. Maniac always worries about his big-end; always worries about everything. Some biker.

I'd better explain all these nicknames, before you think I'm potty. Geronimo's name is really Weston; which becomes Western; which becomes Indian chief; which becomes Geronimo. Carpet's real name is Matt; but he says when he was called Matt everybody trampled on him. Some chance. Carpet's a big hard kid; but he'd always help out a mate in trouble. Mani-

61

ac's really called Casey equals crazy equals Maniac. Got it?

Anyway, Geronimo himself comes over laughing, having just fastened the Club secretary to his chair by the back-buckles of his leathers, and everyone's pissing themselves laughing, except the secretary who hasn't noticed yet...

'You game?' asks Geronimo.

I was game. There was nowt else going on except ten kids doing an all-male tribal dance right in front of the main amplifier of the disco. The rest had reached the stage where the big joke was to pour somebody's pint into somebody else's crash-helmet. Besides, it was a privilege to go anywhere with Geronimo; he could pull laughs out of the air.

'Half an hour; Sparwick chippie,' said Geronimo, and we all made tracks for home. I managed seventy up the main street, watching for fuzz having a crafty fag in shop-doorways. But there was nobody about except middle-aged guys in dirty raincoats staring in the windows of telly-shops. What's middle age a punishment for? Is there no cure?

At home, I went straight to my room and got my tent and sleeping-bag. Don't know why I bothered. As far as Geronimo was concerned, a tent was just for letting down the guy-ropes of, on wet nights. And a sleeping-bag was for jumping on, once somebody got into it. I raided the larder and found the usual baked beans and hot dogs. My parents didn't eat either. They bought them for me camping, on condition that I didn't nick tomorrow's lunch.

Stuck me head in the lounge. Dad had his head stuck in the telly, worrying about the plight of the

Vietnamese boat-refugees. Some treat, after a hard week's work!

'Going camping. Seeya in morning.'

'Don't forget your key. I'm not getting up for you in the middle of the night if it starts raining.'

Which really meant I love you and take care not to break your silly neck 'cos I know what you're going to get up to. But he'd never say it, 'cos I've got him well trained. Me Mum made a worried kind of grab at the air, so I slammed down the visor of me helmet and went, yelling 'Seeya in morning' again to drown her protests before she made them.

Moon was up, all the way to Sparwick chippie. Making the trees all silver down one side. Felt great, 'cos we were *going* somewhere. Didn't know where, but *somewhere*. Astronaut to Saturn, with Carpet and Geronimo... and Maniac? Well, nobody expected life to be perfect...

Carpet was there already. 'What you got?' he said, slapping my top-box.

'Beans an' hot dogs. What you got?'

'Hot dog an' beans.'

'Crap!'

'Even that would make a change.'

'No, it wouldn't. We have that all week at the works canteen.'

We sat side by side, revving-up, watching the old grannies in their curlers and carpet-slippers coming out of the chippie clutching their hot greasy packets to their boobs like they were babies, and yakking on about who's got cancer now.

'If I reach fifty, I'm goin' to commit suicide,' said Carpet.

'Forty'll do me.'

'Way you ride, you won't reach twenty.'

Maniac rode up, sounding like a trade-in sewing-machine. He immediately got off and started revving his bike, with his helmet shoved against his rear forks.

'What's up?

'Funny noise.'

'No funnier than usual,' said Carpet. But he took his helmet off and got Maniac to rev her again, and immediately spotted it was the tins in Maniac's top-box that were making the rattling. 'Bad case of Heinz,' he muttered to me, but he said to Maniac, 'Sounds like piston-slap. We'd better get the cylinder-head off . . .'

Maniac turned as white as a sheet in the light from the chippie, but he started getting his tool kit out, 'cos he knew Carpet knew bikes.

Just as well Geronimo turned up then. Carpet's crazy; he'd sooner strip a bike than a bird . . .

'Where to then?' said Geronimo.

Nobody had a clue. Everybody had the same old ideas and got howled down. It's like that sometimes. We get stuck for a place to go. Then Maniac and Carpet started arguing about Jap bikes versus British, and you can't sink lower than that. In a minute they'd start eating their beans straight from the tins, tipping them up like cans of lager. Once the grub was gone, there'd be no point to going anywhere, and I'd be home before midnight and Dad would say was it morning already how time flies and all that middle-aged smartycrap.

And Geronimo had lost interest in us and was watching the cars going past down the main road. If something interesting came past worth burning off, like a Lamborghini or even a Jag XJ12, we wouldn't see him again for the rest of the night.

So I said I knew where there was a haunted abbey. I felt a bit of a rat, 'cos that abbey was a big thing with Dad. He was a mate of the guy who owned it and he'd taken me all over it and it was a fascinating place and God knew what Geronimo would do to it . . . But we'd got to go somewhere.

'What's it haunted by?' Geronimo put his helmet against mine, so his voice boomed. But he was interested.

'A nun. There was a kid riding past one night, and this tart all clad in white steps out right under his front wheel and he claps his anchors on but he goes straight into her and arse over tip. Ruins his enamel. But when he went back there was nothing there.'

'Bollocks,' said Geronimo. 'But I'll go for the sex-interest. What's a nun doing in an *abbey*?' He was no fool, Geronimo. He could tell a Carmelite from a camshaft when he had to.

'Ride along,' he said, and took off with me on his shoulder, which is great, like fighter-pilots in the war. And I watched the street-lights sliding curved across his black helmet, and the way he changed gear smart as a whip. He got his acceleration with a long hard burst in second.

I found them the abbey gate and opened it and left it for Maniac to close. 'Quiet – there's people living here.'

'Throttle-down,' said Geronimo.

But Maniac started going on about the abbey being private property and trespass; a real hero.

'Have a good trip home,' said Geronimo. 'Please drive carefully.'

Maniac flinched like Geronimo'd hit him. Then mumbled, 'O.K. Hang on a minute, then.'

Everybody groaned. Maniac was a big drinker, you see. Shandy-bitter. Lemonade. He'd never breathalyse in a million years. But it made him burp all the time, like a clapped-out Norton Commando. And he was always having to stop and go behind hedges. Only he was scared to stop, in case we shot off without him. That time, we let him get started, and *went*. Laughing so we could hardly ride, 'cos he'd be pissing all over his bulled-up boots in a panic.

It was a hell of a ride, 'cos the guy who owned the abbey kept his drive all rutted, to discourage people like us. Geronimo went up on his foot-rests like a jockey, back straight as a ruler. Nobody could ride like Geronimo; even my Dad said he rode like an Apache.

It was like scrambling; just Geronimo's straight back and the tunnel of trees ahead, white in the light of Geronimo's quartz-halogen, and the shining red eyes of rabbits and foxes staring out at us, then shooting off. And our three engines so quiet, and Maniac far behind, revving up like mad, trying to catch up. I wished it could go on for ever till a sheet of water shot up inside my leathers, so cold I forgot if I was male or female . . .

Geronimo had found a rut full of water, and soaked me beautifully. He was staring back at me, laughing through his visor. And here was another rut coming up. Oh, hell – it was lucky I always cleaned my bike on Saturday mornings. Anyway, he soaked me five

66

times, but I soaked him once, and I got Carpet twice. And Maniac caught up; and then fell off when Carpet got *him*. And then we were at the abbey.

A great stretch of moonlit grass, sweeping down to the river. And the part the monks used to live in, which was now a stately home, away on the right all massive and black, except where our lights shone on hundreds and hundreds of windows. And the part that used to be the abbey church was on the left. Henry the Eighth made them pull that all down, so there was nothing left but low walls, and the bases of columns sticking out of the turf about as high as park benches, like black rotten teeth. And at the far end of that was a tall stone cross.

'That's the Nun's Grave,' I said. 'But it's not really. Just some old bits and pieces of the abbey that they found in the eighteenth century and put together to make a good story...'

'Big'ead,' said Geronimo. 'Let's have a look.' He climbed on to the base of the first column; and, waving his arms about, leapt for the base of the second column. Screaming like a banshee. 'I AAAAAMM the Flying Nun.' It was a fantastic leap; about twelve feet. He made it, though his boots scraped heavily on the sandstone blocks. I shuddered, and looked towards the house. Luckily, there wasn't a light showing. Country people went to bed early. I hoped.

'I AAAAAAAAMMM the Flying Nun,' wailed Geronimo, 'and I'm in LOOOOOOVE with the Flying Abbot. But I'm cheating on him with the Flying Doctor.'

He attempted another death-defying leap, missed his footing, and nearly ruined his married future.

'Amendment,' said Carpet. 'He *was* the Flying Nun.'

'Never fear. The Flying Nun will fly again,' croaked Geronimo from the grass. His helmet appeared to have turned back-to-front, and he was holding his crotch painfully.

'Amendment,' said Carpet. 'The Flying Soprano will fly again.'

We were all so busy falling about (even Maniac had stopped worrying about trespass) that we didn't see the bloke at first. But there he was, standing in the shadow of his great house, screaming like a nut-case.

'Hooligans! Vandals!' Sounded like he was having a real fit.

'Is that that mate of yours?' Carpet asked me.

'Mate of my Dad's,' I said.

'Your Dad knows some funny people. Is he an out-patient, or has he climbed over the wall?' Carpet turned to the distant raging figure and amiably pointed the two fingers of scorn.

He shouldn't have done that. Next second, a huge four-legged shape came tearing towards us over the grass. Doing a ton with its jaws wide open and its rotten great fangs shining in the moonlight. It didn't make a sound; not like an ordinary dog. And the little figure by the house was shouting things like, 'Kill, kill, kill!' He didn't seem at all like the guy I met when my Dad took me round the house . . .

Maniac turned and scarpered. Geronimo was still lying on the grass trying to get his helmet straight. And the rotten great dog was making straight at him. I couldn't move.

But Carpet did. He ran and straddled over Geronimo. Braced himself, and he was a big lad; there was thirteen stone of him.

The dog leapt, like they do in the movies. Carpet thrust his gauntleted fist right up its throat. Carpet rocked, but he didn't fall. The dog was chewing on his glove like mad, studs and all.

'Naughty doggy,' said Carpet reprovingly, and gave it a terrific clout over the ear with his other hand.

Two more clouts and the dog stopped chewing. Three, and it let go. Then Carpet kicked it in the ribs. Sounded like the big bass drum.

'Heel, Fido!' said Carpet.

The dog went for Geronimo, who was staggering to his feet; and got Carpet's boot again. It fell back, whimpering.

The next second, a tiny figure was flailing at Carpet. 'Leave my dog *alone*. How *dare* you hit my dog. I'll have the RSPCA on you – that's all you hooligans are good for, mistreating dogs.' He was literally foaming at the mouth. 'I don't know what this country's coming to . . .'

'It's going to the dogs,' said Carpet. He pushed the man gently away with one great hand, and held him at arm's length. 'Look, mate,' he said sadly, wagging one finger of a well-chewed gauntlet, 'take the Hound of the Baskervilles home. It's time for his Meaty Chunks . . .'

'I am going,' spluttered the little guy, 'to call the police.'

'I would, mate,' said Carpet. 'There's a highly dangerous dog loose round here somewhere . . .'

The pair of them slunk off. Maniac returned from

the nearest bushes to the sound of cheers. Geronimo slapped Carpet on the shoulder and said 'Thanks, mate,' in a voice that had me green with envy. And we all buggered off. After we had ridden three times round the house for luck. Including the steps in the formal garden.

'There's another way out,' I said, 'at the far end.'

The far drive seemed to go on forever. Or was it that we were riding slowly, because Carpet was having trouble changing gear with his right hand. I think the dog had hurt him right through the glove; but that was not something Carpet would ever admit.

Just before we went out through the great gates, with stone eagles on their gateposts, we passed a white Hillman Imp, parked on the right well off the road, under the big horse-chestnut trees of the avenue. It seemed empty as we passed, though, oddly enough, it had its sunshields down, which was a funny thing to happen at midnight.

Outside, Geronimo held up his right hand, US Cavalry-fashion, and we all stopped.

'Back,' said Geronimo. 'Lights out. Throttle-down. Quiet.'

'What?'

But he was gone back inside. All we could do was follow. It was lucky the moon was out when he stopped. Or we'd all have driven over him and flattened him.

'*What*?' we all said again.

But he just said, 'Push your bikes.'

We all pushed our bikes, swearing at him.

'Quiet!'

The white Hillman glimmered up in the moonlight.

'Thought so,' said Geronimo. A white arm appeared for a moment behind the steering wheel and vanished again.

Maniac sniggered.

'You can't *do* it,' said Carpet. 'Not in a Hillman Imp!'

'You have a wide experience of Hillman Imps?' asked Geronimo.

'Let's stay and watch,' said Maniac.

Carpet and I looked at Geronimo uneasily.

'What do you think *I* am?' said Geronimo, crushing Maniac like he was a beetle. 'Mount up, lads. Right. Lights, sound, music, enter the villain.'

Four headlamps, three of them quartz-halogen, coned in on the Imp. I noticed it was L-reg. It shone like day, but for a long moment nothing else happened.

Then a head appeared; a bald head, with beady eyes and a rat-trap mouth. Followed by a naked chest, hairy as a chimpanzee. The eyes glared; a large fist was raised and shaken.

'Switch off,' said Geronimo. 'And *quiet*.'

We sat and listened. There was the mother and father of a row going on inside the Imp.

'Drive me *home*!'

'It was nothing. Just a car passing. They've gone now.'

We waited; the voices got lower and lower. Silence.

'Start your engines,' said Geronimo. '*Quietly*.'

'What for?' asked Maniac plaintively.

'You'll see,' said Geronimo, and laughed with pure delight.

He and Carpet and me had electric starter-motors;

which of course started us quietly, first press of the button. Good old Jap-crap. Maniac, buying British and best, had to kick his over and over again.

'I'm going to buy you a new flint for that thing,' said Carpet.

Maniac's bike started at last.

'Lights,' said Geronimo.

There was a wild scream; then an even wilder burst of swearing. The bald head reappeared. The car-lights came on; its engine started and revved.

'*Move*!' shouted Geronimo, curving his bike away between the tree trunks.

'Why?' yelled Maniac.

'He'll never live to see twenty,' said Carpet, as we turned together through the branches, neat as a pair of performing dolphins.

Then the Imp was after us, screeching and roaring in second gear fit to blow a gasket.

We went out of those gates like Agostini, down through the slumbering hamlet of Blackdore and up towards the moors. We were all riding four-hundreds, and we could have lost the Imp in ten seconds. But it was more fun to dawdle at seventy, watching the Imp trying to catch up. God, it was cornering like a lunatic, right over on the wrong side of the road. Another outpatient got over the wall. Even more than most motorists, that is.

And old Maniac was not keeping up. That bloody British bike of his; that clapped-out old Tiger was missing on one rotten cylinder.

He was lagging further and further behind. The Imp's lights seemed to be drawing alongside his. He was riding badly, cowering against the hedge, not leav-

72

ing himself enough room to get a good line into his corners. I knew how he'd be feeling; mouth dry as brickdust; knees and hands shaking almost beyond control.

Then the Imp did draw alongside, and made a tremendous side-swipe at him, trying to knock him off into the hedge at seventy. The guy in the Imp was trying to kill Maniac. And there was nothing we could do. I pulled alongside Carpet and pointed behind. But Carpet had seen already and didn't know what to do either.

Then Geronimo noticed. Throttled back, waved us through. In my rear-view mirror I watched him drop further and further back, until he seemed just in front of the Imp's bumper. Up went his two fingers. Again and again. He put his thumb to his nose and waggled his fingers. I swear he did – I saw them in silhouette against the Imp's lights; though afterwards Carpet made out I couldn't have done and that it was something I made up.

At last, the Imp took notice; forgot Maniac cowering and limping beside the hedge, and came after Geronimo.

'Out to the left,' gestured Carpet, and we shot off down a side-road, turned and came back behind the lunatic's car.

So we saw it all in comfort. Oh, Geronimo could have walked away from him; Geronimo could do a hundred and ten if he liked. But just as he was going to, he saw this riding school in a field on the left, on the outskirts of the next village, Chelbury. You know the kind of place – all white-painted oildrums

73

and red-and-white striped poles where little female toffs try to learn to show-jump.

In went Geronimo. Round and round went Geronimo. Round the barrels, under the poles. And round and round went the Imp. Into the barrels and smashing the poles to smithereens. He couldn't drive for toffee – like a mad bull in a china shop and Geronimo the bull-fighter. *Boing, boing, boing* went the drums. Splinter, splinter, splinter in the moonlight went the poles.

Geronimo could have gone on forever. But lights were coming on in the houses; curtains being pulled back on the finest display of trick-riding the villagers of Chelbury will ever see – not that they'd have the sense to appreciate it.

Just as Maniac turned up, minus a bit of paint, we heard the siren of the cop-car. Some toffee-nosed gent had been on the phone.

Of course the cop-car, bumping across the grass through the shambles, made straight for Geronimo; the fuzz always blame the motorcyclist and the Imp had stopped its murder-attempts by that time.

'You young lunatic,' said the fuzz getting out, 'you've caused damage worth thousands . . .'

Geronimo gestured at his bike, which hadn't a scratch on it in the cop-car's headlights. Then he nodded at the Imp, which had four feet of striped pole stuck inside its front bumper.

Then the fuzz noticed that the guy at the wheel was completely starkers. And that there was a long-haired blonde on the back seat trying to put her jumper on inside-out and back-to-front. The fuzz kept losing his grip on the situation every time the blonde

74

wriggled. Well, they're human too. All very enjoyable . . .

We got back to Carpet's place about seven, still laughing so much we were wobbling all over the road. We always end up at Carpet's place after a night out. It's a nice little detached bungalow on top of a hill. And we always weave round and round Carpet's Dad's crazy-paving, revving like mad. And Carpet's Mum always throws open the one upstairs window and leans out in her blue dressing-gown, and asks what the hell we want. And Geronimo always asks, innocent-like, 'This is the motorway cafe, isn't it?' And Carpet's Mum always calls him a cheeky young tyke, and comes down and lets us in and gives us cans of lager and meat pies while she does a great big fry-up for breakfast. And we lie about till lunchtime with our boots on the furniture, giving her cheek, and she's loving it and laughing. I used to wonder why she put up with us, till I realised she was just that glad to have Carpet back alive.

And that was our night out.

On Monday night, when I got home from work, Dad took me in the front room alone. I knew something was up. Had the guy from the abbey rumbled us? But Dad gave me a whisky, and I knew it was worse.

He told me Geronimo was dead; killed on his bike. I wouldn't believe it. No bastard motorist could ever get Geronimo.

Then he told me how it happened. On a bend, with six-foot stone walls either side. Geronimo was coming home from work in the dark. He'd have been tired. He was only doing fifty; on his proper side, two feet out from the kerb. The police could tell from the skid-marks.

The car was only a lousy Morris Marina. Overtaking on a blind corner. The driver didn't stop; but the other driver got his number. When the police breathalysed him, he was pissed to the eyeballs.

I believed it then; and I cried.

We gave him a real biker's funeral. A hundred and seventy bikes followed him through the town, at ten miles an hour, two by two. I've never seen such disciplined riding. Nobody fell off; though a few of the lads burned their clutches out. We really pinned this town's ears back. They know what bikers are now; bikers are *together*.

The Pope died about that time. The Pope only had twelve motorbike outriders; Geronimo had a hundred and seventy. If he met the Pope in some waiting-room or other up above, Geronimo would have pointed that out. But laughing, mind. He was always laughing, Geronimo.

Afterwards, we all went back to the Club and got the drinks in. Then there was a bloody horrible silence; the lads were really down, like I've never seen them. It was terrible.

Then Fred, the Club secretary, gets to his feet and points at the pool table, where Geronimo used to sit, putting the players off their stroke by wriggling his backside.

'If he was standing there,' said Fred, 'if he could see you now, d'you know what he'd say? He'd say "What you being so piss-faced for, you stupid

76

nerks?" ' And suddenly, though nobody saw or heard anything, he *was* there, and it was all right. And everybody was falling over themselves to tell Geronimo-stories and laughing.

We all went to the court-case too, all in our gear. The Clerk of the Court tried to have us thrown out; but one or two of us have got a few O-Levels, and enough sense to hire our own lawyer. Who told the Clerk of the Court where he got off. We were all British citizens, of voting age, as good as anybody else. Har-har.

And the police proved everything against the driver of the Marina. He lost his licence, of course. Then the judge said six months' imprisonment.

Then he said sentence suspended for two years . . .

Why? 'Cos he belonged to the same golf-club as the judge? 'Cos he was middle-aged and big and fat with an expensive overcoat and a posh lawyer?

The lads gave a kind of growl. The Clerk was shaking so much he couldn't hold his papers. So was the Marina driver, who'd been whispering and grinning at his lawyer till then.

The Clerk began shouting for silence; going on about contempt of court. Fred got up. He's sixteen stone of pure muscle, and he's about forty-five with a grown-up son in the Club.

'Not contempt, your honour. More disgust, like.'

I think the lads might have gone too far then. But Geronimo's Mum (she looked very like him) put her hand on Fred's arm and asked him to take her home. And when Fred went we all followed; though a few fingers went up in the air behind backs.

Maniac and Carpet and me tried going on riding

together. But it didn't work out. Whenever we rode together, there was a sort of terrible hole formed, where Geronimo should be. Maniac went off and joined the Merchant Navy, 'cos he couldn't stand this town any more. He still sends Carpet and me postcards from Bahrain and Abu Dhabi (clean ones too!). And we put them on the mantelpiece and forget them.

Carpet and I went on riding; even bought bigger bikes. I still see him sometimes, but we never stop for more than two minutes' chat.

But when I ride alone, that's different. You see you can't hear very much inside your helmet, when your engine's running. And the helmet cuts down your view to the side as well. So when we need to talk to each other on the move, we have to pull alongside and yell and yell. And when you first notice a guy doing that, it often comes over funny. Well, I keep thinking I hear him; that he's just lurking out of the corner of my eye. I just know he's somewhere about; you *can't* kill someone like Geronimo.

I got engaged last week. Jane's a good lass, but she made one condition. That I sell my bike and buy a car. She says she wants me to live to be a grandfather. And when my Mum heard her say it, she suddenly looked ten years younger.

So I'm taking this last ride to the abbey in the moonlight, and I've just passed Sparwick's chippie. And the moon is making one side of the trees silver, and I'm *going* somewhere. Only I'm not going with Geronimo; I'm getting further away from Geronimo all the time. Nearer to the old grannies with their hair in curlers coming out of the chippie clutching their hot greasy bundles. The middle-aged guys staring in the telly-shop windows.

And I'm not sure I like it.

The Creatures in the House

DAWN broke over Southwold seafront.

The wind was blowing against the waves; white horses showed all the way to the horizon; smaller and smaller as if painted by some obsessional Dutch marine artist. On the horizon itself sat a steamship, square as a pan on a shelf, scarcely seeming to move.

Seafront deserted; beach-huts huddled empty in the rain. The only movement was a flaking flap of emulsion-paint on the pier pavilion, tearing itself off in the wind.

Miss Forbes opened her eyes on her last day. Eyes grey and empty as the sea. She eased her body in the velvet reclining rocker in the bay window; luxurious once, now greased in black patches from the day and night shifting of her body. It was some years since she had been to bed. Beds meant sheets and sheets meant washing . . . She seldom left the bay window. She took her food off the front doorstep and straight on to the occasional table by her side. Once a week she took the remains to the dustbin. Otherwise there were just the trips to the toilet, and the weekly journey to the dripping tap in the kitchen for a pink-rosed ewerful of water. She opened her eyes and looked at the sea and wondered what month it was. Her mind was clearer this morning than for a long time. The creature in the house had not fed on her mind for a week. There wasn't much of Miss Forbes' mind left to feed on. A few shreds of memory from the forties; a vague guilt at things not done. The creature itself was weakening. The creature knew a time would come soon when it had nothing to feed on at all. Then it would have to hibernate, like a dormouse or hedgehog. But first the creature must provide for its future, while there was still time. There was something Miss Forbes had to do . . .

She rose shakily, after trying to straighten thick stockings of two different tones of grey. She went out into the hall, picked up the 1968 telephone directory, and, her eyes squinting two inches off the page, looked up the solicitor's number.

She had difficulty making the solicitor's girl understand who she was; an old-standing client and a wealthy one. She mentioned the name of partner after partner . . . old Mr Sandbach had been dead twenty years . . . young Mr Sandbach retired last spring. Yes, she supposed Mr Mason would have to do . . . eleven o'clock?

Then she slowly climbed the stairs, slippered feet carving footprints in dust thicker than the worn stair-carpet. In what had once been her bedroom she opened the mirrored wardrobe door, not even glancing at her reflection as it swung out at her.

She began to wash and comb and dress. With spells of sitting down to rest it took three hours. The creature had to lend her its own waning strength. Even then, Miss Forbes scarcely managed. The creature itself nearly despaired.

But between them, they coped. At half past ten, Miss Forbes rang for a taxi, the ancient black stick-phone trembling in her hand.

The taxi-driver watched her awestruck in his rear-view mirror. Two things clutched tightly in her gloved hand. A door-key and big lump of wallpaper with something scrawled on the back in a big childish hand. Like all his kind, he was good at reading things backwards in his mirror.

'I leave all my worldly possessions to my niece, Martha Vickers, providing she is unmarried and living alone at the time of my death. On condition that she agrees, and continues, to reside alone at 17 Marine Parade. Or if she is unable or unwilling to comply with my wishes, I leave all my possessions to my great-niece, Sarah Anne Walmsley . . .'

The taxi-man shuddered. *He'd* settle for a heart-attack at seventy . . .

'Suppose I spend all the money, sell the house and run?' asked Sally Walmsley. 'I mean what's to stop me?'

'Me, I'm afraid,' said Mr Mason, wiping the thick fur of dust off the hallstand of 17 Marine Parade, and settling his plump pinstriped bottom. 'We are the executors of your aunt's estate . . . we shall have to keep *some* kind of eye on you . . . it could prove unpleasant . . . I hope it won't come to that. Suppose you and I have dinner about once every six months and you tell me what you've been up to . . .' He smiled tentatively, sympathetically. He liked this tall thin girl with green eyes and long black hair. 'Of course, you

82

could contest the will. It wouldn't stand up in court a moment. I couldn't *swear* your aunt was in her right mind the morning she made it. Not of sound testamentary capacity as we say. But if you break the will, it would have to be shared with all your female aunts and cousins – married and unmarried. You'd get about three thousand each – not a lot.'

'Stuff *them*,' said Sally Walmsley. 'I'll keep what I've got.' She suddenly felt immensely weary. The last six months had happened so fast. Deciding to walk out of art school. Walking out of art school. Trailing London looking for work. Getting a break as assistant art editor of *New Woman*. And then lovely Tony Harrison of Production going back to his fat, frigid suburban cow of a wife. And then this . . .

'I must be off,' said Mr Mason, getting off the hallstand and surveying his bottom for dust in the spotted stained mirror. But he lingered in the door, interminably, as if guilty about leaving her. 'It was a strange business . . . I've dealt with a lot of old ladies but your aunt . . . she looked . . . faded. Not potty, just *faded*. I kept on having to shout at her to bring her back to herself.

'The milkman found her, you know. When the third bottle of milk piled up on her doorstep. He always had the rule to let three bottles pile up. Old ladies can be funny. She might have gone away. But there she was, sitting in the bay window, grey as dust.

'He seems to have been her only human contact – money and scribbled notes pushed into the milk bottles. She lived on what he brought – bread, butter, eggs, yoghurt, cheese, orange juice. She seems to have never tried to cook – drank the eggs raw after cracking them into a cup.

'But she didn't die of malnutrition . . . the coroner said it was a viable diet, though not a desirable one. Didn't die of hypothermia, either. It was a cold week in March, but the gas fire was full on, and the room was like an oven . . .' He paused, as if an unpleasant memory had struck him. 'In fact, the coroner couldn't find any cause of death at all. He said she just seemed to have faded away . . . put down good old natural causes. Well, I must be off. If there's any way I can help . . .'

Sally nearly said, 'Please don't go.' But that would have been silly. So she smiled politely while he smiled too, bobbed his head and left.

Sally didn't like that at all. She listened to the silence in the house, and her skin crawled.

A primitive man, a bushman or aborigine, would have recognised that crawling of the skin. Would have left the spot immediately. Or if the place had been important to him, a cave or spring of water, he would have returned with other primitive men and performed certain rituals. And then the creature would have left.

But Sally simply told herself not to be a silly fool, and forced herself to explore.

The library was books from floor to ceiling. *Avant-garde* – fifty years ago. Marie Stopes, Havelock Ellis, the early Agatha Christie, Shaw and Wells. Aunt Maude had been a great reader, a Girton girl, a blue-stocking. So what had she read the last ten years? For the fur of dust lay over the books as it lay over everything else. And there wasn't a magazine or paper in the house. So what had she *done* with herself, never going out, doing all her business by post, never putting stamps on her letters till the bank manager began sending her books of stamps of his own volition. Even the occasional plumber or meter-reader had never seen her; only a phone message and the front door open, with scrawled instructions pinned to it . . .

Aunt Maude might as well have been an enclosed nun . . .

But the house with its wood-planked walls, its red-tiled roof, its white gothic pinnacles, balconies and many bay windows was not in bad shape; nowhere near falling down. Nothing fresh paint wouldn't cure. And there was plenty of money. And the furniture was fabulously Victorian. Viennese wallclocks, fit only for the junkshop twenty years ago, would fetch hundreds now, once their glass cases were cleared of cobwebs, and their brass pendulums of verdigris. And the dining-room furniture was Sheraton; genuine, eighteenth-century Sheraton. Oh, she could make it such a place . . . where people would bother to come, even from London. Everybody liked a weekend by the sea. Even Tony Harrison . . . she thrust the thought down savagely. But what a challenge, bringing the place back to life.

So why did she feel like crying? Was it just the dusk of a November afternoon; the rain-runnelled dirt on the windows?

She reached the top of the house; a boxroom under the roof with sloping ceiling; and a yellow stained-glass window at one end that made it look as if the sun was always shining outside; and the massed brick of the chimney-stacks at the other. A long narrow tall room; a wrong room that made her want to slam the door and run away. Instead, she made herself stand and *analyse* her feelings. Simple, really; the stained glass was alienating; the shape of the room was uncomfortable, making you strain upwards and giving you a humiliating crick in the neck. Simple, really, when you had art school training, an awareness of the psychology of shape and colour.

She was still glad to shut the door, go downstairs to the kitchen with its still-dripping tap, and make herself a cup of tea. She left all the rings of the gas stove burning. *And* the oven. Soon the place was as warm as a greenhouse . . .

In the darkest corner of the narrow boxroom, furthest from the stained-glass window where the sun always seemed to shine, up near the grey-grimed ceiling, the creature stirred in its sleep. It was not the fiercest or strongest of its kind; not quite purely spirit, or rather decayed from pure spirit. It could pass through the wood and glass of doors and windows easily, but it had difficulty with brick and stonework. That was why it had installed Miss Forbes in the bay window; so it could feed on her quickly, when it returned hungry from its long journeys. It fed on humankind, but not all humankind. It found workmen in the house quite unbearable; like a herd of trampling, whistling, swearing elephants. Happy families were worse, especially when the children were noisy. It only liked women, yet would have found a brisk WI meeting an unbearable hell. It fed on women alone; women in despair. It crept subtly into their minds, when they slept or tossed and worried in the middle of the night, peeling back the protective shell of their minds that they didn't even know they had; rather as a squirrel cracks a nut, or a thrush a snail-shell; patient, not hurrying, delicate, persistent . . .

Like all wise parasites it did not kill its hosts. Miss Forbes had lasted it forty years; Miss Forbes' great-aunt had lasted nearer sixty.

Now it was awake, and hungry.

Sally hugged her third mug of tea between her hands and stared out of the kitchen window, at the long dead grass and scattered dustbins of the November garden. The garden wall was fifty yards away, sooty brick. There was nothing else to see. She had the conviction that her new life had stopped; that her clockwork was running down. I could stand here for ever, she thought in a panic. I must go upstairs and make up a bed; there was plenty of embroidered lavendered Edwardian linen in the drawers. But she hadn't the energy.

I could go out and spend the night in a hotel. But which hotels would be open, in Southwold in November? She knew there was a phone, but the Post Office had cut it off.

Just then, something appeared suddenly on top of the sooty wall, making her jump. One moment it wasn't there; next moment it was.

A grey cat. A tom-cat, from the huge size of its head and thickness of shoulder.

It glanced this way and that; then lowered its forefeet delicately down the vertical brick of the wall, leapt, and vanished into the long grass.

She waited; it reappeared, moving through the long grass with a stalking lope so like a lion's and so unlike a cat indoors. It went from dustbin to dustbin, sniffing inside each in turn, without hope and without success. She somehow knew it did the same thing every day, at the same time. It had worn tracks through the grass.

'Hard luck,' she thought, as the cat found nothing. Then spitefully, 'Sucker!' She hated the cat, because its search for food was so like her own search for happiness.

The cat sniffed inside the last bin unavailingly, and was about to depart, empty-handed.

'Welcome to the club,' thought Sally bitterly.

It was then that the hailstorm came; out of nowhere, huge hailstones, slashing, hurting. The tom-cat turned, startled, head and paw upraised, snarling as if the hailstorm was an enemy of its own kind, as if to defend itself against this final harshness of life.

Sally felt a tiny surge of sympathy.

It was almost as if the cat sensed it. It certainly turned towards the kitchen window and saw her for the first time. And immediately ran towards her, and leapt on to the lid of a bin directly under the window, hailstones belting small craters in its fur, and its mouth open; red tongue and white teeth exposed in a silent miaow that was half defiance and half appeal.

You can't let this happen to me.

It made her feel like God; the God she had often screamed and wept and appealed to; and never had an answer.

I am *kinder* than God, she thought in sad triumph, and ran to open the kitchen door.

The cat streaked in, and, finding a dry shelter, suddenly remembered its dignity. It shook itself violently, then shook the wetness off each paw in turn, as a kind of symbol of disgust with the weather outside, then began to vigorously belabour its shoulder with a long pink tongue.

But not for long. Its nose began to twitch; began to twitch quite monstrously. It turned its head, following the twitch, and leapt gently on to the kitchen table, where a packet lay, wrapped in paper.

A pound of mince, bought up in the town earlier, and forgotten. Sally sat down, amused, and watched. All right, she thought, if you can get it, you can have it.

The cat tapped and turned the parcel, as if it were a living mouse. Seemed to sit and think for a moment, then got its nose under the packet and, with vigorous shoves, propelled it to the edge of the table, and sent it thumping on to the stone floor.

It was enough to burst the paper the butcher had put round it. The mince splattered across the stone flags with all the gory drama of a successful hunt. The cat leapt down and ate steadily, pausing only to give Sally the occasional dark suspicious stare, and growling under its breath.

OK, thought Sally. You win. I'd never have got round to cooking it tonight, and there isn't a fridge . . .

The cat extracted and hunted down the last red crumb, and then began exploring the kitchen; pacing along the work-tops, prying open the darkness of the cupboards with an urgent paw.

There was an arrogance about him, a sense of

taking possession, that could only make her think of one thing to call him.

When he finally sat down, to wash and survey her with blank dark eyes, she called softly, 'Boss? Boss?'

He gave a short and savage purr and leapt straight on to her knee, trampling her about with agonising sharp claws, before finally settling in her lap, facing outwards, front claws clenched into her trousered knees. He was big, but painfully thin. His haunches felt like bone knives under his matted fur. The fat days must be in the summer, she thought sleepily, with full dustbins behind every hotel. What do they do in November?

He should have been an agony; but strangely he was a comfort. The gas stove had made the room deliciously warm. His purring filled her ears.

They slept, twisted together like symbiotic plants, in a cocoon of contentment.

The creature sensed her sleep. It drifted out of the boxroom and down the intricately carved staircase, like a darkening of the shadows; a dimming of the faint beams that crept through the filthy net curtains from a distant street-lamp.

Boss did not sense it, until it entered the kitchen. A she-cat would have sensed it earlier. But Boss saw it; as Sally would never see it. His claws tightened in Sally's knee; he rose up and arched his back and spat, ears laid back against his skull. Sally whimpered in her sleep, trying to soothe him with a drowsy hand. But she didn't waken . . .

Cat and creature faced each other. Boss felt no

fear, as a human might. Only hate at an intruder, alien, enemy . . .

And the creature felt Boss's hate. Rather as a human might feel a small stone that has worked its way inside a shoe. Not quite painful; not enough to stop for, but a distraction.

The creature could not harm Boss; their beings had nothing in common. But it could press on his being; press abominably.

It pressed.

Boss leapt off Sally's knee. If a door had been open, or a window, Boss would have fled. But no door or window was open. He ran frantically here and there, trying to escape the black pressure, and finally ended up crouched in the corner under the sink, protected on three sides by brickwork, but silenced at last.

Now the creature turned its attention to Sally, probing at the first layer of her mind.

Boss, released, spat and swore terribly.

It was as if, for the creature, the stone in the shoe had turned over, exposing a new sharp edge.

The creature, exploding in rage, pressed too hard on the outer layer of Sally's mind.

Sally's dream turned to nightmare; a nightmare of a horrible female thing with wrinkled dugs and lice in her long grey hair. Sally woke, sweating.

The creature was no longer there.

Sally gazed woozy-eyed at Boss, who emerged from under the sink, shook himself, and immediately asked to be let out the kitchen door. Very insistently. Clawing at the woodwork.

Sally's hand was on the handle, when a thought struck her. If she let the cat out, she would be *alone*.

The thought was unbearable.

She looked at Boss.

'Hard luck, mate,' she said. 'You asked to be let in. You've had your supper. Now bloody earn it!'

As if he sensed what she meant, Boss gave up his attempts on the door. Sally made some tea; and conscience-stricken, gave Boss the cream off the milk. She looked at her watch. Midnight.

They settled down again.

Three more times that night the creature tried. Three times with the same result. It grew ever more frantic, clumsy. Three times Sally had nightmares and woke sweating, and made tea.

Boss, on the other hand, was starting to get used to things. The last time, he did not even stir from Sally's knee. Just lay tensely and spat. The black weight of the creature seemed less when he was near the human.

After three a.m. cat and girl slept undisturbed. While the creature roamed the stairs and corridors, demented. Perhaps it was beginning to realise that one day, like Miss Forbes and Miss Forbes' great-aunt, it too, might simply cease to exist; like the corpse of a hedgehog, by a country road, it might slowly blow away into particles of dust.

A weak morning sunlight cheered the dead grass of the garden. Sally opened a tin of corned beef and gave Boss Cat his breakfast. He wolfed the lot, and then asked again to be let out, with renewed insistence.

Freedom was freedom, thought Sally sadly. Besides, if he didn't go soon there was liable to be a nasty accident. She watched him go through the grass, and gain the top of the wall with a magnificent leap.

Then he vanished, leaving the world totally empty.

She spent four cups of coffee and five fags gathering her wits; then opened her suitcase, washed at the kitchen sink, and set out to face the world.

It wasn't bad. The sky was pale blue, every wave was twinkling like diamonds as it broke on the beach, and her brave new orange Mini stood parked twenty yards down the road.

But it was Boss she watched for; in the tangled front garden; on the immaculate lawn of the house next door.

Then she looked back at number 17, nervously. It looked all right, from here . . .

'Good morning!' The voice made her jump.

The owner of number 16 was straightening up from behind his well-mended fence, a handful of dead brown foliage in one hand.

He was everything she disliked in a man. About thirty. Friendly smile, naive blue eyes, check shirt, folk-weave tie. He offered a loamy paw, having wiped it on the seat of his gardening trousers.

'Just moved in then? My name's Mike Taverner. Dwell here with my mama . . .'

Half an hour later she broke away, her head spinning with a muddling survey of all the best shops in town and what they were best for. The fact that Mr Taverner was an accountant and therefore worked gentleman's hours. That he was quite handy round the house and that anything he could do ... But it was his subtly pitying look that was worst.

Stuff him! If *he* thought that *she* was going to ask *him* round for coffee ...

She spent the day using Miss Forbes' money. A huge hand-torch for some reason; a new transistor radio, satisfyingly loud; a check tablecloth; three new dresses, the most with-it that Southwold could offer. She ordered a new gas stove, and gained the promise that the Post Office would re-connect tomorrow ...

She still had to come home in the end.

She put her new possessions on the kitchen table, all in a mass, and they just seemed to shrink to the size of Dinky Toys. The silence of the house pressed on her skin like a cold moist blanket.

But she was firm. Went upstairs and made the bed in the front bedroom with the bay window. Then sat over her plate of bacon and eggs till it congealed solid, smoking fag after fag. The sounds that came out of the transistor radio seemed like alien code messages from Mars.

She went to bed at midnight, clutching the radio under one arm, and fags, matches, torch, magazines with the other.

But before she went, she left the kitchen window open six inches. And a fresh plate of mince on the sill. It was like a hundred-to-one bet on the Grand National ...

Boss left the house determined never to return, and picked up the devious trail through alley and garden,

94

backyard and beach-shelter that marked the edge of his territory. Smelling his old trademarks and renewing them vigorously, he stalked and killed a hungry sparrow in one alley; found some cinder-embedded bacon rind in another, but that was all. He was soon hungry again.

By the time dusk was falling, and he rendezvoused at the derelict fishermen's hut with his females, he was very hungry indeed. The memory of the black terror had faded; the memory of the raw mince grew stronger.

He sniffed noses and backsides with one of his females in particular, a big scrawny tortoiseshell with hollow flanks and bulging belly. But he could not settle. The memory of the mince grew to a mountain in his mind; a lovely blood-oozing salty mountain.

Around midnight, he got up and stretched, and headed out again along his well-beaten track.

Ten yards behind, weak and limping, the tortoiseshell followed. She followed him further than she had ever ventured before; but she was far more hungry than him; her plight far more desperate. And she had smelt the rich raw meat on his breath . . .

The creature felt them enter the house; now there were two sharp stones in its shoe.

It had been doing well before they came. Sally had taken two Mogadon, and lay sleeping on her back, mouth open and snoring, a perfect prey. The creature was feeding gently on the first layer of her mind; lush memories of warmth and childhood, laughter and toys. First food in six months.

Uneasy, suddenly it fed harder, too hard. Sally moaned and swam up slowly from her drugged sleep;

95

sat up and knew with terror that something precious had been stolen from her; was missing, gone for ever.

The creature did not let go of her; hung on with all its strength; it was so near to having her completely.

Sally felt as cold as death under the heaped blankets; the sheets were like clammy winding-sheets, strangling, smothering. She fought her way out of them and reeled about the room, seeking blindly for the door in the dark. Warm, she must get warm or . . .

The kitchen . . . gas stove . . . warm. Desperately she searched the walls for the door, in the utter dark. Curtains, windows, pictures swinging and falling under her grasping hands. She was crying, screaming . . . Was there no door to this black room?

Then the blessed roundness of the door handle, that would not turn under her cold-sweating palm, until she folded a piece of her nightdress over it. And then she was going downstairs, half-running, half-falling, bumping down the last few steps on her bottom, in the dim light of the street-lamp through the grimy curtains . . .

The whole place rocked still in nightmare, because the creature still clung to her mind . . .

Twice she passed the kitchen door, and then she found it and broke through, and banged the light on.

Check tablecloth; suitcase; tweed coat. Sally's eyes clutched them, like a drowning man clutches straws. The creature felt her starting to get away; struggling back to the real world outside.

But much worse, the creature felt two pairs of eyes glaring; glaring hate. The tom-cat was crouched on the old wooden draining-board, back arched. But the tom was not the worst. The she-cat lay curled on a pathetic heap of old rags and torn-up newspaper under the sink. And her hatred was utterly immovable. And there were five more small sharp stones now in the creature's shoe. A mild squeaking came from within the she-cat's protective legs. Little scraps of blind fur, writhing . . .

Sally's mind gave a tremendous heave and the creature's hold broke. The creature could not stand the she-cat's eyes, alien, blank, utterly rejecting.

It fled back up the stairs, right to the boxroom, and coiled itself in the dark corner, between a high shelf and the blackened ceiling.

It knew, as it lapsed into chaos, that there was one room in its house where it dared never go again.

Back in the kitchen, Sally closed the door and then the window, and lit all the rings of the gas stove. The tom-cat shook itself and rubbed against her legs, wanting milk.

'Kittens,' said Sally, 'kittens. Oh you *poor* thing.'

But at that moment there was nothing in the world she wanted more than kittens. She put on a saucepan, and filled it to the brim with milk.

She felt Boss stir on her knee towards dawn. She opened her eyes, and saw him on the windowsill, asking to go out.

'All right,' she said reluctantly. She opened the window. She knew now that he would come back. Besides, the purring heap of cat and kittens, now installed on a heap of old curtains in an armchair, showed no sign of wanting to move. She would not be alone . . .

She left the window open. It was not a very cold night, and the room was now too hot if anything, from the gas stove.

She was wakened at eight, by Boss's pounding savage claws on her lap. He made loud demands for breakfast.

And he was not alone. There was a black-and-white female sitting washing itself on the corner of the table; and a white-and-ginger female was curled up with the mother and kittens, busy washing all and sundry. The aunties had arrived.

'Brought the whole family, have you?' she asked Boss sourly. 'Sure there aren't a few grandmas you forgot?'

He gave a particularly savage purr, and dug his claws deeper into her legs.

'OK,' she said. 'How would Tyne-Brand meat loaf do? With pilchards for starters?'

By the time they had finished, the larder was bare. They washed, and Sally ate toast and watched them washing. She thought, I'm bonkers. Only old maids have cats like this. People will think I'm mad. The four cats regarded her with blankly friendly eyes. Somehow it gave her courage to remember the nightmare upstairs . . .

Then the cats rose, one by one. Nudged and nosed each other, stretched, began to mill around.

It reminded her of something she'd once seen; on telly somewhere.

Lionesses, setting off to hunt. That was it. Lionesses setting off to hunt.

But for God's sake, they'd *had* their breakfast . . .

Boss went to the door and miaowed. Not the

kitchen door; the door that led to the nightmare staircase. Mother joined him. And Ginger. And the black-
and-white cat she'd christened Chequers.

When she did not open that door, they all turned
and stared at her. Friendly; but expectant. Com-
pelling.

My God, she thought. They're going hunting whatever is upstairs. And inviting me to join in . . .

They were the only friends she had. She went; but
she picked up Boss before she opened the door. He
didn't seem to mind; he settled himself comfortably
in her arms, pricking his ears and looking ahead. His
body was vibrating. Purr or growl deep in his throat.
She could not tell.

The she-cats padded ahead, looked at the doors of
the downstairs rooms, then leapt up the stairs. They
nosed into everything, talking to each other in their
prooky spooky language. They moved as if they were
tied to each other and to her with invisible strands of
elastic; passing each other, weaving from side to side
like a cat's cradle, but never getting too far ahead, or
too far apart.

They went from upstairs room to upstairs room,
politely standing aside as she opened each door. Leaping on to dust-sheeted beds, sniffing in long-empty
chamber pots.

Each of the rooms was empty; dreary, dusty, but
totally empty. Sally wasn't afraid. If anything, little
tingling excitements ran through her.

The cats turned to the staircase that led to the
boxroom in the roof. They were closer together now,
their chirrups louder, more urgent.

They went straight to the door of the narrow room,

with the yellow stained-glass window that was always sunshine.

Waited. Braced. Ears back close to the skull.

Sally took a deep breath and flung open the door.

Immediately the cold came, the clammy winding-sheet cold of the night before. The corridor, the stairs twisted and fell together like collapsing stage scenery.

She would have run; but Boss's claws, deep and sharp in her arm, were more real than the cold and the twisting; like an anchor in a storm. She stood. So did the cats, though they crouched close to the floor, huddled together.

Slowly, the cold and twisting faded.

The cats rose and shook themselves, as after a shower of rain, and stalked one by one into the boxroom.

Trembling, Sally followed.

Again the sick cold and twisting came. But it was weaker. Even Sally could tell that. And it didn't last so long.

The cats were all staring at the ceiling at the far end; at a dark grey space between the heavy brick-work of two chimneys; between the ceiling and a high wooden shelf.

Sally stared too, But all she could see was a mass of cobwebs; black rope-like strands blowing in some draught that came through the slates of the roof.

But she knew her enemy, the enemy who had stolen from her, was there. And for the first time, because the enemy was now so small, no longer filling the house, she could feel anger, red healthy anger.

She looked round for a weapon. There was an old short-bristled broom leaning against the wall. She put down Boss and picked it up, and slashed savagely at the swaying cobwebs, until she had pulled every one of them down.

They clung to the broomhead.

But they were only cobwebs.

Boss gave a long chirrup. Cheerful, pleased, but summoning. Slowly, in obedience, the three she-cats began to back out of the door, never taking their green eyes from the space up near the ceiling.

Sally came last, and closed the door.

They retired back to the kittens, in good order.

Back in the boxroom, the creature was absolutely still. It had learned the bitter limitations of its strength. It had reached the very frontier of its existence.

It grew wise.

Back in the kitchen, there came a knock on the door.

It was Mr Taverner. Was she all right? He thought he had heard screams in the night . . .

'It was only Jack the Ripper,' said Sally with a flare of newfound spirit. 'You're too late – he murdered me.'

He had the grace to look woebegone. He had quite a nice lopsided smile, when he was woebegone. So she offered him a cup of coffee.

He sat down and the she-cats climbed all over him, sniffing in his ears with spiteful humour. Standing on his shoulders with their front paws on top of his head . . . He suffered politely, with his lopsided grin. 'Have they moved in on you? Once you feed them, they'll never go away . . . they're a menace round

Southwold, especially in the winter. I could call the RSPCA for you . . .?'

'They are *my* cats. I *like* cats.'

He gave her a funny look. 'They'll cost you a bomb to feed . . .'

'I know how much cats cost to feed. And don't think I can't afford to keep a hundred cats if I want to.'

Again he had the grace to shut up.

Things went better for Sally after that. Mike Taverner called in quite often, and even asked her to have dinner with his mother. Mrs Taverner proved not to be an aged burden, but a smart fifty-year-old who ran a dress-shop, didn't discuss hysterectomies, and watched her son's social antics with a wry long-suffering smile.

The kittens grew; the house filled with whistling workmen; the Gas Board came finally to install the new cooker.

And Sally took to sleeping on the couch of a little breakfast room just off the kitchen; where she could get a glimpse of sea in the mornings, and the cats came and went through the serving-hatch.

She slept well, usually with cats coming and going off her feet all night. Sometimes they called sharply to each other, and there was a scurrying of paws, and she would waken smoothly. That noise meant the creature from the boxroom was on the prowl.

But it never tried anything, not with the cats around.

And every day, Sally and the cats did their daily patrol into enemy territory. What Sally came to think of, with a nervous giggle, as the bearding of the boxroom.

But the creature never reacted. The patrols became almost a bore, and pairs of cats could be heard chasing each other up and down the first flight of stairs, on their own.

What a crazy life, Sally thought. If Mike Taverner *dreamt* what was going on, what would he say? Once, she even took him on a tour of the house, to admire the new decorations. Took him right into the box-room. All the cats came too.

The creature suffered a good deal from Mike's elephantine soul and great booming male voice . . .

But the boundary between victory and defeat is narrow; and usually composed of complacency.

The last night started so happily. Mike was coming to dinner; well, he was better than *nothing*. Sally, in her newest dress and butcher's apron, was putting the finishing touches to a sherry trifle. A large Scotch sirloin steak lay wrapped in a bloody package on the fridge, handy for the gas cooker.

Sally had just nipped into the breakfast room to lay the table when she heard a rustling noise in the kitchen . . .

She rushed back in time to see Boss nosing at the bloody packet.

She should have picked him up firmly; but chose to shoo him away with a wild wave of her arms. Boss, panicking, made an enormous leap for the window. The sherry trifle, propelled by all the strength of his back legs, catapulted across the room and self-destructed on the tiled floor in a mess of cream and glass shards a yard wide.

Sally went berserk. Threw Boss out of the back door; threw Chequers after him, and slammed the window in Mother's face, just as Mother was coming in.

That only left the kittens, eyes scarcely open, crawling and squeaking in their basket. She would have some peace for once, to get ready.

Maybe Mike was right. Too many cats. Only potty old maids had so many cats. RSPCA . . . good homes.

She never noticed that the kittens had ceased to crawl and squeak and maul each other. That they grew silent and huddled together in one corner of their basket, each trying desperately to get into the middle of the heap of warm furry bodies . . .

She scraped and wiped up the trifle. Made Mike an Instant Whip instead. In a flavour she knew he didn't like. Well, he could lump it. Sitting round her kitchen all day, waiting to have his face fed. Fancy living with *that* face for forty years . . . growing bald, scratching under the armpits of his checked shirt like an ape. He'd only become interested in her seriously when he heard about her money . . . Stuff him. Better to live alone . . .

Mike was unfortunate to ring up at that point. He was bringing wine. Would Châteauneuf-du-Pape do? How smug he sounded; how sure he had her in his grasp.

He made one of his clumsy teasing jokes. She chose to take it the wrong way. Her voice grew sharp. He whinged self-righteously in protest. Sally told him what she *really* thought of him. He rang off in high dudgeon, implying he would never bother her again.

Good. Good riddance to bad rubbish. Much better living on her own in her beautiful house, without a great clumsy corny man in it . . .

But his rudeness had given her a headache. Might as well take a Mogadon and lie down. She suddenly felt cold and really tired . . . sleep it off.

Boss was crazy for the sirloin; Mother was very worked-up about her kittens; and the window-catch was old and rusted. Five minutes' work had the window open. Mother made straight for her kittens and Boss made straight for the meal. Three heaves and he had the packet open, and the kitchen filled with the rich smell of blood. Ginger and Chequers appeared out of nowhere and Mother, satisfied her brood was safe, rapidly joined them in a baleful circle round the fridge.

They were not aware of the creature, in their excitement. It was in the breakfast room with Sally, behind a closed door and feeding quietly.

But Boss was infuriatedly aware of the other cats, as they stretched up the face of the fridge, trying to claw his prize out of his mouth. He sensed he would have no peace to enjoy a morsel. So, arching his neck magnificently to hold the steak clear of the floor, he leapt down, then up to the windowsill and out into the night.

Unfortunately, it was one of those damp nights that accent every odour; and the faintest of breezes was blowing from the north towards the town centre of

Southwold. Several hungry noses lifted to the fascinating new scent.

Within a minute, Boss knew he was no longer alone. Frantically he turned and twisted through his well-known alleyways. But others knew them just as well, and the scent was as great a beacon as the circling beams of Southwold's lighthouse. Even the well-fed domestic tabbies, merely out for an airing, caught it. As for the hungry desperate ones...

Boss was no fool. He doubled for home. Came through the window like a rocket, leaving a rich red trail on the yellowed white paintwork, and regained the fridge. Another minute, and there were ten strange cats in the room. Two minutes and there were twenty.

Boss leapt for the high shelving in desperate evasion. A whole shelf of pots and pans came down together. The noise beggared description, and there were more cats coming in all the time.

Next door the creature, startled, slipped clumsily in its feeding. Sally came screaming up out of nightmare and ran for the warmth of her kitchen, the creature still entangled in her mind.

To the creature, the kitchenful of cats was like rolling in broken glass. Silently, it fled to the high shelf in the boxroom.

It was unfortunate for the creature that Boss had very much the same thought. The hall door was ajar. He was through it in a flash and up the stairs, the whole frantic starving mob in pursuit.

Back in the near-empty kitchen, there came a thunderous knocking on the door. It burst open to reveal Mr Taverner in a not-very-becoming plum-coloured smoking-jacket. He flung his arms round Sally, demanding wildly to know what the matter was.

Sally could only point mutely upstairs.

By the time they got there, Boss, with slashing claws and hideous growls that filtered past the sirloin steak, was making his last stand in the open boxroom door.

And, confused and bewildered by so many enemies, weak from hunger and shattered by frustration, the creature was cowering up on its shelf, trying to get out into the open air through the thick brickwork of the chimneys. But it was old, old . . .

Boss, turning in desperation from the many claws dabbing at his steak, saw the same high shelf and leapt.

Thirty pairs of ravening cat-eyes followed him.

The creature knew, for the first in its ancient existence, how it felt to be prey . . .

It lost all desire to exist.

Nobody heard the slight popping noise, because of the din. But suddenly there was a vile smell, a rubbish-tip, graveyard, green-water smell.

And the house was empty of anything but dust and cobwebs, woodlice and woodworm. Empty for ever.

Sea-coal

I was painting me seven-hundredth railing. In wi' the
scraper, ripping off the faded blue flakes, scattering
them like flowers on the sick January grass. Again, I
heard the echo of Granda's voice.

'If you're doing owt, son, mek a job of it.'

Granda even made a job of dying. Torpedoed twice
in the war, but Jerry couldn't kill him. Fell off a ladder
at the age of seventy-nine, painting his own guttering.
A stroke, the doctor said. Dead before he hit the
ground.

Christ, I miss him.

I eased my muscles, looked back along all the railings I'd done, stretching down the hill. Glad they were
bright orange, brave against the grey January sky, the
grey works, grey steam billowing from grey chimneys.
Making a lot of steam the works was, but not much
chemical. Hardly a feller in sight. Rationalisation,
they said, redeployment. Ha bloody ha. That works
had been the town's Big Mammie for a hundred years.
Fat pay-packets and all the copper wire you could
nick, smuggled out wrapped round your belly under
your shirt.

Big Mammie's sick, maybe dying. Keep on painting
the railings; stops you going bonkers.

Six months back, when we'd just left school and were rotting on the dole, they'd really conned us wi' Job Creation. Moving into the realm of new technology, gaffer said first morning, his spectacles winking shifty under the neon-lights. How to live at peace wi' the computer! Chance of a real job at the end, if you showed the makings!

We really lapped it up, that first morning, in our shining bright safety-helmets. Overalls so new they argued back as you walked. First lunchtime we swaggered down the shops wearing the lot; clattering our boots till we drove the old granny in the off-licence mad. We are the ICI boys!

Once, I even got a chance to help a fitter wi' a faulty pump. And a fitter is what I want to be. The pump was small, shiny, beautiful piece of craftsmanship. I put my head close to it an' listened, like Granda used to. Which noise was the fault? The thin tapping at the top, or the wheezing like bronchitis in the round, curly middle?

'What yer reckon?' I asked the fitter. That's how fitters talk to each other.

'What yer mean, what yer reckon?' He had a little sneaky putting-down grin on his face.

'What's up wi' pump?'

'Aah don't give two damns. It's coming out, that's all aah know.'

He cut the power wi' a red button; turned a yellow wheel to cut off the flow of chemical. Started undoing the pump's screws. One stuck. He took a hammer to it. The shining metal dented, crumpled, collapsed in a wreck. 'Bloody German rubbish,' said the fitter, pulling the wrecked pump free and throwing it on a trolley. 'Get that packing-case open, kid, will you? Wi'out breaking what's inside, right?'

Inside was another pump, exactly the same.

'Why didn't we mend the old one?'

'Cheaper to buy new. Pumps is cheaper than fitters.'

'Me Granda . . .'

'Your Granda went down wi' the *Titanic*, kid! This is *today*.'

'Call yerself a *fitter*?' I shouldn't ha' said it; but he shouldn't ha' said that about Granda. He thought about clouting me one, then noticed me size. He kicked the pump instead, like it was a dead cat, and wheeled it away.

The next week, the pound started climbing against the dollar. The Americans stopped buying chemical. The works starting making steam instead. The bosses started walking round like they were going to their own funeral, and we were all put on painting railings . . .

There were eight of us, wi' a foreman, painting the railings round a wood next the works. Within a week, Bowlby began pissing about, snapping the thin branches off the chemically poisoned trees and throwing them into the soupy yellow river. The foreman caught him an' played hell. Bowlby just laughed an' went right on doing it. Soon all the rest were doing it, an' the foreman didn't come round much any more, except wi' the packets on payday.

I tried larkin' about wi' them once; but it made me feel like a little kid, so I jacked it in. There's no point in going backwards. But they went on wi' it. I'd seen

110

them through the trees, lighting fires, roasting stolen tatties, toasting sandwiches, like chimpanzees in safety-helmets. Sometimes they shouted I was licking foreman's arse, but I ignored them and they soon got tired.

I was halfway down my seven-hundred-an'-first railing when I heard the noise they were making change; their voices went quieter, a creepy sort of gloating. I tried to ignore it, but I knew they were going to hurt something. Something worse than trees. Not me, mind. I'm big, and when I land somebody one . . .

Finally, I couldn't bear it. I stuck me brush back in the paint and walked towards their sodding fire. One or two of them saw me, and ran ahead through the trees, shouting I was coming.

Bowlby had a cat; a poor thin white thing; from the look on his face, he wasn't thinking of feeding it sandwiches. He had a bit o' rope round its neck. It had its ears back, terrified but still hopeful. It licked his hand.

So it was me an' Bowlby again. It always was. The rest o' the kids were nowt, shadows hanging round the edges.

'What you doing wi' cat?'

'None of your business.'

'I'll mek it my business.' I looked round the rest. They kept their eyes down. One had a brick in his hand. So they were going to drown the cat. Coulda' been worse. Bowlby'd roast a cat alive . . .

'I'll tek that cat.'

Bowlby watched me coming. I began to think that

the poor cat was the cheese in the trap; an' I was the poor bloody mouse.

'C'mon, mek me,' said Bowlby. I'd have been scared, but for his eyes. They were rovin' all over the place, half cocky, half doubtful. Telegraphing, Granda called it.

I moved in on him. I tell you, I was pig-sick wi' six months o' painting railings. Just lookin' for something to smash that needed smashing. Like Bowlby. But I was scared of hurting the cat . . .

He threw it in my face. A good trick, but for his telegraph-eyes. And I don't play goalie for nowt. I had that poor cat snatched left-handed against my chest and still had time to see Bowlby's kick coming.

I grabbed his foot and just held it there, giving it the odd twist for good luck. Then I pushed the foot up an' back.

He kept his feet, just. At the cost of running backwards about fifteen feet like something out of Laurel and Hardy. Trouble was it carried him back to the steep, slippery river-bank, and down he went in a slather of foam, like a depth charge exploding in the Yellow Sea.

I laughed myself sick; a shit like Bowlby where he belonged at last. Just in time, I realised nobody else was laughing. Next second, they were all on me. I'd never have thought they had it in them. But they meant it, boots an' all.

I managed. I had to punch one-handed, wi' the cat. But I stood back an' punched big – a couple o' golden handshakes they won't forget. But they just stood back then, an' started throwing things.

I turned me back on them, and walked off through

112

the wood. One stone rattled on me helmet, but they didn't follow. Maybe they were givin' Bowlby the kiss o' life.

I kept walking, blind wi' misery. It wasn't just me bruises; it was suddenly knowing how much they hated me, how they'd planned the whole thing. And the bloody railings, and even that was coming to an end and then it'd be the dole again an' lying in bed till children's telly started, trying to think of some reason for getting up. Even school would've been better. And I'd left me flask and sandwiches back there. An' Mam wouldn't let me take the cat home an' the stupid thing would go back to the wood an' the next time they'd do it in for sure. I just hated the whole of bloody 1982 and I wished to hell I was somewhere else, anywhere . . .

So I never really grasped how I got out o' the far side o' the wood and into that slum. Never seen a slum like it. They were so poor they couldn't even afford telly; not an aerial in sight. The houses were the usual Coronation Street, but they'd made no efforts, not even a lick o'paint. The streets were cobbles; the gutters full o' dirty soapy water and little kids were playing in them wi' matchbox-boats, wi' a match for a mast an' a little bit o' paper for a sail. They got up an' stared at me open-mouthed as I walked past. They had big boots an' maroon jerseys that buttoned at the neck an' skinhead haircuts and trousers that hardly covered their knees. Stared at me like I was a Martian, snot hanging from their noses that they wiped on the cuffs o' their jumpers, and great big shadowed eyes. I

113

felt embarrassed, a bit. I suppose I did look funny, walking along wearing a safety-helmet an' carrying a cat. But I hung on to the cat. I had a feeling that if I let go, it wasn't long for this world. It was thin as razor blades, and shivering in great convulsive shivers. Nothing that a month of home-cooking wouldn't cure but . . .

Where was home? I hadn't a clue. Never been down this part of town in me life. The street-name said 'Back Brannen Street'. Never heard of it. There were four men on the corner, squatting on their haunches, wearing caps, looking like Norman Wisdom multiplied by four.

'Excuse me,' I said, staring down at them.

'Yes, kidder?' asked one, kindly.

'I've got meself a bit lost.'

'Ye're a bit big for that. Where'd ye want, kidder?'

'I live on the Marden Estate,' I said stiffly.

'Marden Estate? Never heard on it. Hev ye, Jackie?'

Another man shook his head. 'Aah've heard of Lord Redescape's Estate and Sir Percy Hambly's Estate. Never heard of Marden Estate. Heard of Marden Farm mind – very good place for sheep, is Marden Farm. D'you like roast mutton, kidder?' They all laughed, like there was a private joke they weren't letting on about.

'Marden Farm's near us,' I said, 'except it was demolished afore I was born. We still got Marden Farm Road.'

'*Demolished*?' asked the first man. 'That's a staff-officer's word for ye, Jackie! Last thing aah saw *demolished* was a German strongpoint in Thiepville Wood.'

He brought a worn tobacco-tin out of his pocket, and took out a squashed flat dog-end. With loving care he pressed it back into shape. The tobacco inside rustled dryly. Then he took a pin from his coat-lapel, stuck it through the dog-end and lit up, turning his head carefully sideways, so he didn't burn his nose. He took one drag, and passed it to his mate. I watched as they solemnly passed it round the circle like an Indian pipe of peace. Holding it by the pin; it had burnt down to a quarter of an inch long, too small to hold between their fingers.

'D'you wanna fag?' I burst out, horribly embarrassed. Took twenty king-size from my overalls and flipped it open.

They stared. 'Jesus God!' said one. They didn't move. Just stared at the packet of twenty like they'd never seen one before. I grabbed five out of the packet and thrust them into the first man's hand, where it lay on his crouching knees.

He looked at me. 'Who are ye, hinny? Carnegie?'

It was all so strange, I ran.

As I turned the corner, I heard their mocking voices, calling like birds.

'Thank you, Carnegie.'

But round the corner was worse. A man sat on a doorstep, propped against the door. A fat man with no legs. Instead, he had big round black leather pads where his legs should be; held on by leather straps fastened round his waist. His fat face lifted, as he heard me running. His eyes were covered with small round dark glasses.

'Buy a box of matches, mate?'

I wanted to go on running, but a kind of nosy

horror took me up to him. There was a flimsy wooden tray hanging round his neck by a piece of white tape. On it were nine boxes of matches. On the front of the tray was written DISABLED – THREE CHILDREN. There was a greasy cap on the pavement beside him, guarded by an old black dog, nearly as fat as the man.

'Help a wounded soldier, mate?' he said, in a sing-song voice like a worn gramophone record. 'Wife and three kids. Military Medal and bar.' He pointed to the breast of his cut-down blue coat. There were four faded medal-ribbons and a silver badge. His whole face strained towards me, through the round black spectacles. 'Help an Old Contemptible, mate, what caught it at Wipers!'

I reached desperately into my overalls, and tossed two ten-pence pieces into his cap. His face frowned at the double-clink. He scrabbled for the coins, felt their milled edges; bit them. Then he said,

'Two florins. God bless you, mate.' I turned to go, but his big, warm hand reached out and clasped mine. 'Don't forget your box of matches, mate. And give us a hand up – it's me dinner-time.' Suddenly he had both big hands on my shoulders, and was heaving himself upright on to the black leather pads. I had to brace my free hand against the wall to stop myself being pulled over on top of him. His breath, his warmth, the smell of his overcoat, were like a farm animal's.

'Thanks, mate.' He released me, and reached down for his cap, steadying his tray of matches with a practised hand. How could he be practised at having no legs? How could he exist, and even think of dinner, with no legs?

Unbearable. I ran, the safety-helmet bouncing like a pan on my head, the cat digging its claws into me, clinging on tight.

'You forgot your matches, mate!' I looked back; he was following me, walking slowly on his leather pads, matchbox held aloft.

I ran up a side-alley. And another, and another. I ran a long time. When I came to myself, the alley had turned into a cinder-track between allotments. The allotments had funny high fences, made of the rough bark off pine trees, but in weird, wriggly shapes, full of knot-holes. There was a dripping tap, fastened to a wooden post, quite alone on a corner. Dripping gently on the cinders. I suddenly felt very thirsty; my mouth felt like a desert of alkali.

I was still guzzling when I heard a voice say, 'You'd better leave a bit of water for the plants.' I looked up, dribbling water from my mouth over the cat's fur. Expecting another monster.

But he wasn't a monster. He was a young bloke – bit older than me. Thin, but in a ruddy-faced, fit sort of way. Bright, blue, friendly eyes, and a big ginger moustache, neatly trimmed. The only weird thing about him was his clothes – a battered suit with waistcoat and watch-and-chain. No collar an' tie, only a spotless white muffler. His cap, another Norman Wisdom special, was pushed well back on his ginger curls, and he was leaning over his allotment gate, smoking a pipe. The thin blue smoke curled up in the calm air, and he looked totally contented. It was just funny, him being dressed like some old-age pensioner, and yet looking so young.

117

'Cat could do wi' a square meal,' he said. 'Why not give it an Oxo cube?'

'Just rescued it,' I said. 'Some kids were goin' to drown it.'

'Got a few scraps.' He opened his gate, as slowly and grandly as if he was the Duke of Newcastle.

Mind you, even the Duke of Newcastle wouldn't have minded owning what was inside. A long path of old brick stretched into the distance, through three trellis archways hung wi' pink roses. The well-raked soil bulged with healthy-looking flowers, better than my dad ever managed; all in well-drilled rows like soldiers on parade. There was a pigeon-cree, painted in green and white stripes, with ornate fretwork on top, full of plump cooing pigeons. Further on, through the third trellis, vegetables. Turnips like cannonballs; cabbages like even bigger cannonballs. Hoed lines of potatoes. A tarred black hut, then a greenhouse full of thin-stemmed tomatoes, with yellow fruit.

My God, all this in January . . . and that explained everything, the hollow-eyed kids, the man with no legs.

I was dreaming.

Now I'm good wi' dreams, 'cos I dream a lot. And I've learnt to control them. If they start turning into a nightmare, I can wake up. But this dream, at the moment, was OK, so I let it be.

'We haven't been introduced,' said the moustached guy, suddenly all stiff and formal. 'Name's Billy Dack – put it there.' He had a grip like a warm six-inch vice.

'Mike Anderton,' I said, recovering my hand and flexing it behind my back, to restore the circulation.

118

He fetched a crumpled packet of grease-proof paper, and began spilling out crusts and white pork-fat on the brick path for the cat. The cat lowered its tail, and ate with a desperate gulping motion.

'No breakfast,' said Billy, 'like three million others. You in work then or still at school?'

'Job Creation,' I said with a grimace, 'painting railings.'

'You've not starved, though. Ye're a big lad for your age. Not shavin' yet? Ye look fit enough for a gentleman . . . Like to give me a hand?'

He pointed to a five-foot cylinder of rusting iron that stood by the greenhouse. All chimneys and levers and furnace-doors, like a little brother to Stephenson's *Rocket*.

'What the hell is it?' I asked.

He frowned thunderously. 'Watch yer language, son. Or I'll mek ye wash your mouth out wi' soap.' His blue eyes were very sharp; he looked like he thought he had the right to wash out my mouth with soap. Ah, well, what did it matter in a dream?'

'What is it?' I said, swallowing a sharp crack.

'It's an old donkey-boiler,' he said, 'off a ship. I'm fitting it into the greenhouse, to keep it warm, come winter.'

'I'll give you a hand,' I said. We struggled it into the greenhouse, and connected it to the hot-water system somehow, even though the two things weren't meant for each other. He dragged out what he called his box o' bits – lead piping, old brass taps, great hanks of wire, old tin-openers, screws and nuts – a whole packing-case full. I watched him heat bits of metal red-hot in the stove of his hut, and hammer them into shape like a blacksmith.

'Are you a blacksmith?'

'Shipyard fitter,' he said. 'Till they sacked me, the minute aah finished me apprenticeship. They're building ships wi' apprentices now, they can't afford to employ grown men.'

We finished; he packed his box o' bits away. 'Each bit o' that could tell its own story,' he said. 'Never throw owt away, then ye'll never lack for owt. Well, aah reckon ye've earned a bit o' bait. Kettle's on.'

We went back to the hut. My, it was snug. Old black kettle singing on the stove. China cups and saucers wi' little rose-buds on them. Curtains at the window, and even a bunk wi' a patchwork quilt. He saw me looking at the bunk.

'Aah sleep here in the summer, for a bit o' peace and quiet. There's ten of us in three rooms, back home. Not room to swing a cat.'

He looked into the teapot. It was half full of soggy tea-leaves. 'Aye, I think that'll stand one more fill.' When he poured the tea out, after a lot of stirring, it was as pale as lager; but he spooned two sugars into my cup without asking, and trailed in long strings of condensed milk from a sticky brown tin. It tasted great. Then he took down a tin with Japanese women painted all over it, carrying sunshades, but most of them were worn away. He held it out to me.

It was full of stale, broken cakes. But he looked at me with the grand smile of a king, like he was giving me a real treat, so I took one.

'Aah load the bread carts for a baker every morning. Only takes an hour, and he gives me all yester-

120

day's leftovers. Keeps our family in bread an' cakes all week.' He bit with gusto into a vicious-coloured green triangle. My cake tasted like sawdust wi' pink icing, but he was watching, so I ate it.

'Good, eh?' he said. That's the best cake the baker does. You're a good chooser! And, by the bye, what ye got yourself apprenticed as a painter for? From the way ye helped me wi' that boiler, ye'd make a canny fitter.'

'I want to be a fitter,' I spluttered, still battling wi' the sawdust.'

'Then why don't you? Painting's a softy's job. They're signing on apprentices at the North-eastern Marine – all they can lay their hands on. They'll sack ye at twenty-one, like they sacked me. But ye'd have a trade, an' things can't go on being bad forever.'

'Me granda served his time at the North-eastern Marine. Goodwin Anderton he was called.

'Aah knew a Goodwin Anderton there,' said Billy. 'But he was an apprentice wi' me – a lad my age.'

We stared at each other in growing silence. There just couldn't be two men called Goodwin Anderton – never in the history of the world . . .

I took a deep breath and asked shakily, 'What's the date, Billy?'

He reached for a pile of newspapers he kept handy for lighting the stove.

'Twenty-third of July – no, that's last Tuesday's – the twenty-sixth of July.' The paper he was holding up was the *Daily Mail. But it was twice the size it should be.*

'What year?' I shouted.

'1932, of course.'

121

'Oh, all right,' I said to myself. 'I'm dreaming and I don't like this dream any more. Wake up.' I closed my eyes and willed myself to wake up as usual. All I got was a totally undreamlike pain on my shin. I opened my eyes, to see him grinning and returning the steel-tipped toe of his boot under his chair.

'That wasn't part of no dream, bonnie-lad.'

He didn't believe me about 1982 at first. But I had a newspaper, too, tucked into the pocket of me overalls. *The Sun.* He examined it with interest, till he got to page three, then he stuffed it straight into the roaring stove.

'Ye mucky-minded little bugger!'

'Everybody reads it where I come from, even me Mam.'

'You must have had a bloody funny bringing-up!'

I distracted him with my digital watch-calculator. Only I had a job to stop him taking the back off to see how it worked. I had to distract him again, wi' a king-sized fag. He lit up with gusto, using a burning piece of paper from the stove.

'Big as a toff's cigar!' He inhaled till the ends of his ginger moustache twitched.

'A toff like Carnegie?' I asked. He nodded.

'Who is Carnegie?'

'American. Biggest millionaire in the world, son. Lights his cigars wi' hundred-dollar bills.' He sounded wistful, as if Carnegie lived in fairyland. And it was that wistfulness that brought it all home to me, that threw me in a panic.

'Billy – I'm caught. If I've travelled in time, how do I get back?'

He eyed me coolly. 'Aah believe ye have. Like that feller in H. G. Wells – the Time Traveller. Come to think of it, you do look a bit like something out of H. G. Wells wi' that hat and that cat. Blimey – I'm a poet an' I don't know it!'

'But how do I get back?' I screeched.

'Aah'll bend me mind to it. Mind you, ye've no cause to grumble, even if ye can't get back. Ye've got a grand new pair o' boots there, that I bet don't let in water, and a watch anybody'd give a thousand pounds for, and enough spare flesh on ye to last three months. Come and help me gather sea-coal for the donkey-boiler, while aah think about your dilemma.'

I didn't notice much on our walk down to the sea; I was too worried. But there was a lot of horses and carts about; big piles of manure in every street. And kids running round in bare feet, though Billy said they preferred it that way in summer. I knew a lot of the houses, but there were gaps between, more green fields. And I saw a man with a wooden leg playing an accordion on the street corner.

The beach was just the same. And the castle on the cliffs. And the swimming pool, though it was brand-new concrete then . . .

The beach was cut in half, as if by a knife. The sunny, southern half was full of holidaymakers in deckchairs. A few, men and women, were wearing striped bathing-costumes that covered them nearly as much as clothes. But most people were sitting there in their Sunday best, hats an' all. There were three dignified men, grand wi' moustache and cap and

123

watch-chain, paddling in the water up to their knees, and still looking like they were going to have a chat wi' King George the Fifth. Somebody had a wind-up gramophone, and a whole crowd had gathered to listen.

The cold, northern end of the beach, shadowed by the cliffs, was nearly empty. Long black bands ran along it, round the high-tide mark. Sea-coal. Washed out of coal seams in the cliffs, by the waves. Washed off the decks of colliers in storms; washed out of wrecked ships over hundreds of years. I'd run across those black bands as a little lad, grumbled when they'd hurt my feet. Never realised what they were.

People here did. Well away from the holiday-makers, creeping like mice, frightened of being noticed and giving offence, crawled a grey stooping army of old women, thin coughing men and little kids. Each with their soaking black bag.

Between the sea-coalers and the holidaymakers, on the very edge of the sunlight, a policeman was stand-ing, sweating in a serge collar done up to his neck.

'One of the toffs complains,' said Billy, 'he'll chuck us all off the beach. Aah wish ye'd left that bloody silly helmet behind. Ye're like something out of *The Shape of Things to Come*. Aah suppose aah should be grateful you've left the bloody cat.'

We got down to it. I followed him along one of the curving black bands, picking up the tiny bits of coal. They were mostly smaller than peas. If you found one as big as a cherry, it was an event. You couldn't scoop them up in handfuls, or you just ended up wi' a sackful o' wet sand. You picked 'em, one by one, like prize strawberries. If you bent down to pick 'em, your back hurt like hell. If you knelt, you got your knees soaked. I sort of went blind by the end, sweat dripping off me nose, just picking, picking. Billy left me far behind.

I carried me sea-coal home on me back. It dripped and made me bottom wet. We'd just got to the allotment gate when Billy said, 'Here's poor Manny Gosling comin'.'

A ghost wavered down that cinder-track, a ghost so thin and staring-eyed that I hoped, I prayed, he'd walk straight past. But Billy said kindly, 'What fettle the day, Manny?'

The ghost halted, swivelled his head. 'Hallo, Marrer. Fair to middlin'.' He pulled a spotless white hanky out of his pocket and began to cough into it. The coughing had a life of its own. The coughs grew bigger and bigger. Manny heaved and shook, as if some enormous, invisible animal had landed on his back and was tearing the life out of him. He clung to a fencepost with his free hand, and the whole fence shook for twenty yards.

Then the white hanky blossomed a little pink rose. Another. Then a bigger red one. Then a whole bunch of roses. Blood and spit trickled down his spotless white muffler.

'Steady on, Manny,' said Billy, gently, putting a strong brown hand over the thin pale hand that clutched the fence. It seemed to help. The coughing got less and less, and finally stopped.

'Better?'

'Better as aah'll ever be, now.'

'Come in for a cup of tea, Marrer.' And Billy

opened the allotment gate as grandly as he'd opened it for me. But Manny wouldn't go into the hut with us.

'I'll stay out here, Billy. There's more fresh air out here.'

'What's up wi' him?' I hissed.

'TB – consumption. He'll never see next spring. First cold east wind'll finish him.

'But *we* can cure TB easy. A few shots of penicillin – piece of cake.'

'Aren't *you* the lucky ones?'

'But if I took him back to our time wi' me . . .'

Billy gave me one of his sharp blue looks.

'You're very sure you're going back, all of a sudden. I thowt ye were stuck . . .'

'I've been thinking . . . if I just go back the way I came . . . it's worth a try.'

'Aye, it's that or nowt. Maybe you came on a return ticket, maybe on a single. There's only one way of finding out. But even if ye are on a return ticket, aah reckon it'll be for one passenger, bonnie-lad, not two.'

'Can I try and get Manny through with me?'

'S'up to ye, bonnie-lad. Nowt to do wi' me.'

'I'd like you there, in case it doesn't work.'

'Aye, well, we'll give Manny his tea, and take him an' all. He could do wi' a brave new world, could Manny.'

We gave Manny his tea. I thought he was going to start coughing again, over the sawdust-cake, but he managed to swallow it. He also managed to totter as far as Back Brannen Street. The legless man was gone, thank God.

126

At the end of Back Brannen Street was a pale blue railing, quite decently painted, with thin-leaved chemically-sick trees behind, that had a familiar look. Billy spoke to a couple of the sunken-eyed kids who were still playing with their matchboxes in the gutter. 'Ye seen this feller before?' he said, pointing to me, all cat and safety-helmet again.

'Yes. He came out of that gate, but we couldn't get in – it's stuck now. It's always stuck.'

I pushed the gate. The cat shivered. The gate opened easily. We passed through, all three of us. Trod on through the silent leafy July trees. The air grew colder; the sky grew grey. Leaves seemed to be falling; at least the trees got more and more bare. Manny shivered, pulling up his jacket collar round his thin neck.

'Aah cannit go no further, Billy.' He sank on to a fallen log. We stood around, awkwardly. Ahead, I was sure I could hear crashings of branches, distant shouts. I thought I saw a glint of firelight through the winter trees; it was coming on dusk.

'*C'mon*, Manny,' I said. 'You must try. Not much further. There's doctors can make you well over there, Manny. Plenty o' food – nobody goes hungry.'

'Sounds like the bleddy kingdom o' heaven,' said Manny, and began coughing again.

I looked at Billy; he gave me a straight look back. 'I can't walk any further either, son. There's something holding us back.' He nodded at the cat, held against my chest. 'Reckon that's your return ticket, son. I think I seen her over our side 'afore. But she's only a ticket for one . . .'

127

I knew what he was thinking. If I let Manny hold the cat, Manny would go and I would stay.

'Aah know where Goodwin Anderton lives,' said Billy. 'He only lives three streets from us. Aah see him nearly every week . . .'

I closed my eyes, and my head swam. Granda. Granda back. Granda young an' strong. A chance to do a real job; build ships instead of painting endless bloody railings. Hitler coming, and the war. Granda survived it, so could I.

I hesitated.

Too long. Manny said, fretful, 'Take us home, Billy. Aah'm catching me death o' cold, sitting here.'

I looked at Billy again, but he was already hauling Manny to his feet.

'Tara, son,' he said, wi'out looking at me. 'Aah'll not tell Goodwin ye called – he's a mate o' mine!' The way he said it, I'd rather he'd hit me.

They didn't seem to be walking very fast, but they vanished quickly amongst the trees, like smoke. At the same moment, the cat jumped out o' me arms and was off. By gum, I was scared then. I ran an' ran, till I was right among that lot at the fire.

'What's up wi' you?' asked Bowlby's mate. 'You look like you seen a ghost.' But Bowlby had knocked off early to get dry, and they weren't in a mood to try anything.

Then, of course, I had to go back; all the way to the gate that led on to Back Brannen Street. Just to make sure I hadn't been dreaming after all.

The gate was still there; it needed painting, thick wi' rust. An' it didn't open when I pushed it.

Beyond? A bloody great open space, with drums of chemical piled under black polythene sheets. All the chemical the company couldn't sell to the Americans. Not a sign of Back Brannen Street . . .

It was all fading, just like a dream. I must've dreamed it all, I told meself, walking home.

Except when Mam made me take me dirty boots off, a little piece of coal fell out of them. No bigger than a pea . . .

The Dracula Tour

Dear Aunty Evelyn,

You may remember that I wrote to your agony column when I was courting George? Well, I took your advice about going out with Frank as well, to broaden my interests, and it worked. They had a terrible fight in the frozen-food depot behind Mecca Dancing and Frank was in hospital three days, but no bones broken thank God. The day Frank got out George popped the question, and it seemed safest to say yes for Frank's sake, and we've been married two years now, but no little ones yet which is not of my choosing!

My parents are very satisfied with George. He got my dad a V-reg Maxi at a price you wouldn't believe, but George says it's being in the Trade. George fixes it for dad on Sunday afternoons, which gives Mum and me a nice chance for a chat. And he's fitted them up a really lovely wrought-iron telephone-shelf in the hall and flushed all the doors. And the goldfish pond he's put them in the garden is a treat, except the cat next door keeps eating the fish and George says the only cure is chicken-wire over the top. But Mum says this will spoil the view and she'd rather have the view than the fish. And George is getting Mum some plastic fish through a friend so all may yet be well.

He has made our home a little palace – he is busy every moment God sends when not working overtime or out with his mates. He built me a little sewing-room behind the kitchen with a fully-fitted bathroom on top (he got the pink bathroom suite from a closing down sale in Manchester). Now he says I ought to go to evening-class to learn sewing. I think I should because he keeps looking at the sewing-room and saying what a smashing workshop it would make. But I'm rather shy and it's hard to take on something new all at once.

My only complaint about George is that he isn't Romantic. We didn't have a honeymoon as George said for that price we could get the latest Aga, and when the honeymoon was just a memory the Aga would still be going strong. While he was installing it during our little honeymoon-at-home, he encouraged me to try my hand at wallpapering, and now George says I am a dab-hand. I have done every room in the house, even papered the ceilings. Now I am doing Mum's house as well because I get a bit lonely with George out at evening-class three nights a week. Last winter he did Electric Wiring, and rewired the whole house, and gave me a lot of additional sockets where he can plug in his Black-and-Decker any time he wants to. The winter before he did Practical Plumbing and we had no bursts, though plenty round here did including Mum and Dad. But George soon fixed that, and they thought the world of him, as some neigh-bours had no toilet for a week which is hard.

But now I find my thoughts straying to Other Men,

131

even George's friend Duggie, when he calls when George is out and decides to wait. Duggie is younger than George and looks just like Robert Redford, except he is six foot four with a little ginger moustache. I sometimes sit next to Duggie on our studio-couch, but all he does is twist his cap in his hands or stir his tea again and tells me how wonderful George is. I'm afraid Duggie thinks the sun shines out of George's backside, just like my Dad. Certainly he's a wonderful provider, he's just not Romantic.

He's only Romantic about Saudi Arabia. Sometimes he talks about going to Saudi for three years and making three hundred quid a week, which would set us up, as there is nothing to spend it on in Saudi, just sand and shit-beetles. (You must excuse me writing that but I want you to have the unvarnished facts.) Then we could have a detached bungalow with two-car garage, and George could teach me to drive before he went back to Saudi.

I said why couldn't I come too – I quite fancied riding a camel even if they did make you seasick. But George said the Saudis have abolished women. And what about the White Slavers who kidnap English wives and sell them in the bazaar in Cairo?

That gave me ever such a funny feeling for weeks after; especially after lunch on weekdays, when George wasn't home. I mean, standing in that bazaar only wearing a gilded bra and see-through gauzy trousers like that Fry's Turkish Delight advert on the telly. And a bearded sheikh sweeping you up on his pommel and carrying you off across the Trackless Desert. And all them hareems! But George says there's nothing there, only sand and shit-beetles.

I didn't believe him. I think he wanted a hareem for himself. So I told Mum, and Dad had a word with George, and George gave up the idea of Saudi, on condition that Dad traded his Maxi for a W-reg Opel Manta in mint condition with twin-carbs, that George wanted to suss out.

But I still get those funny daydreams, especially in the warm weather.

Anyway, I tackled George about being Romantic in the end. This year he wanted to do Deep-Freeze Technology at evening-class, but I said why not do something Romantic to broaden your interests? So he came back saying he'd booked us in for a ten-week course on 'The History of the Horror Movie'. Well, I could have cried; that's not very Romantic, is it? But then I thought if I got scared I could snuggle in and George might put his arm round me and it mightn't be bad.

Till he told me Duggie was coming too.

The first night was awful. This teacher-woman talked and talked and I couldn't understand a word and George and Duggie kept saying, 'What time does Frankenstein start – or is she Frankenstein?' Whispering, but out loud, if you know what I mean. Then the movie started and it was called 'The Sideboard' – or it might have been the Cabinet – 'of Doctor Caligari'. It was all right at first – this ruined abbey and ghostly trees and all swishing mist and two old monks plotting. Then this beautiful girl comes swimming through the mist and one old monk mutters something to the other – in German, then the sub-title comes up:

'THAT IS MY FIANCEE'

Well, I've never heard George laugh so hard – I

thought he was going to do himself a damage and people turned round and began hushing him and George said to one man, 'And up yours and all, mate.' Anyway, I was so ashamed I had to leave and I thought I'd have a coffee in a cafe next to the Tech, so I could see George as they came out, but there were these three fellers in there started eyeing my legs and laughing and egging each other on, so I pretended not to notice. Then I left and went round to Mum's and had a nice cup of tea. You're just not safe these days, anywhere . . .

Anyway, George and me had words, and I told him I wasn't going again and he said seven quid down the drain. I didn't think he and Duggie would go again either, after what they said to that man, but they did and the next week they did Frankenstein. I remember because they came home still arguing and George said it was rubbish making a man out of spare parts and Duggie said a mate of his had built a Ford Cortina out of spare parts nicked from work and put a Rolls-Royce engine into it. But George said, 'Frankenstein's your *organic* mate, and a Cortina's your *inorganic*.' Whatever that means. But it finished the argument, because Duggie didn't know what he was talking about and I don't think George did either.

Next week they came home arguing again. About how you could tell an ash tree from a sycamore of all things, and George said that ash trees had one wing on their seeds, and sycamore two, and that stubbed Duggie out. Then George turns to me and says, 'You can get your bags packed, Missus. We're going to Rumania for Christmas.'

Well, that upset me, because we always go to

134

Mum's. She does the tree so nice, and all the presents beautifully wrapped. I cried a bit, and Duggie had the sense to go home for once and George actually put his arm round me and it was Romantic. So I asked where Rumania was. He said it was nowhere near Saudi. Saudi was all sand and shit-beetles but Rumania was all mountains and fir trees and snow and blizzards and wolves and great. I didn't much like the sound of wolves, but he kept his arm round me and I imagined us riding through the snow on a sleigh drawn by horses and being chased by wolves but George stopped them getting me though they ate some peasants. Including Duggie (who was coming with us as usual). George said he would fix up the sleigh with a feller he knew, once we got there. So I said I'd go, if it was nowhere near Saudi. Mum didn't like the idea, but Dad calmed her down.

Anyway, George went off to Gladstone Woods one night before Christmas, and brought back this branch off an ash tree. Mum was upset, because he usually brings her back a free Christmas tree from Gladstone Woods, and that year Dad had to pay six pounds for one. George spent all that week cutting up that branch, and sharpening each bit at one end, and when I asked him what he was doing he said making tent-pegs. And I said what did we want tent-pegs for, because if we were camping out in all that snow with wolves I wasn't going. He told me we were going to the best Intourist hotel in Transylvania, in a large town called Cluj, which was guaranteed free of wolves and had full central heating and a full English breakfast. So I said what did we want the tent-pegs for, and he said I wasn't to bother my pretty little head. But

I knew they really were tent-pegs because George borrowed a big mallet off my brother Maurice, who's a scoutmaster.

Then Duggie came round and said what about the Holy Water. He'd been to every Catholic church in town and all he'd got was . . . He pulled a sauce bottle out of his pocket, not even the Family size let alone the Jumbo Bargain size. And it was only half full, and there was still tomato-sauce sticking to it. George was rightly scathing, but Duggie said had *he* ever tried borrowing Holy Water with a teaspoon, when the priest might come any minute? George said forget it, he'd buy a litre of topping-up water at Halford's and get a mate of his, a vicar whose car he serviced, to do him a return favour.

Then Duggie said what about the garlic, did George know it had to be wild garlic, fresh-picked? And George said how the hell could he get wild fresh-picked garlic at Christmas, with snow on the ground in England, let alone Rumania? But I was able to help there; I had a little jar of dried garlic, because I once did an evening-class in Exotic Cookery, and still had a bit left as I was always sparing with it as it makes your breath smell like an Italian waiter, especially if you're going on to friends afterwards. And George said go out and buy six more jars, we might as well be on the safe side, dealing with a crafty bastard like that. And I said a crafty bastard like what and he said don't bother your sweet head, love, the crafty sod'll get nowhere near you. And Duggie said the crafty bastard wouldn't fancy a faceful of George's knuckle-pie, let alone a stake through the heart.

Then George gave a loud cough (though he hadn't

a cold) and started talking about snow and sleighs again and told me that 'Transylvania' meant 'through the forests' and I got all romantic feelings again, and stopped listening to what they were talking about.

Anyway, on Christmas Eve we set off for Ringway Airport, to catch the Jumbo for Bucharest in plenty of time. George's friend Frank, the one he put in hospital, drove us across in one of his dad's taxis. It was a Rolls-Royce. Frank kept not looking where he was going and turning round and saying, 'Give the crafty sod one for me.'

'Right up him, squire,' said George. 'But do keep death off the road, drive on the bloody pavement, that's the way.' I never liked the way Frank drives – it's why I could never have married him. But at Ringway he told us the taxi-ride was on the house. His dad would never miss the petrol and they only used the Rolls for funerals anyway ha-ha. I didn't like the way he laughed but it was worse in Customs because the man made George open our suitcase and there was that mallet and those tent-pegs and six jars of garlic and the litre of topping-up water from Halford's.

George told him we were going camping and the man said, 'Whatever turns you on,' and put a cross on the suitcase with a big bit of chalk. Then he opened Duggie's case and it was half-full of beach shirts and brand new jeans that were too wide for Duggie and far too long for George. The man gave all those jeans a funny look.

'You the nervous type, sir?'

Duggie couldn't think of anything to say, but

George tapped the man on the shoulder and asked if he could buy his bit of chalk off him.

'We forgot that,' he said to Duggie. 'It'd come in useful, making crosses on doors and window-frames.'

The Customs man was so nervous he gave George the chalk for nothing.

'Crosses for *what*?' I asked George as we walked across the tarmac. But it wasn't until after take-off, when we had our safety-belts undone and George had a duty-free vodka in each hand, that I found out. The courier came round handing out big black-and-purple stickers. George pulled out our overnight bag, and slapped the sticker on to it. It was a man's face with smarmy hair and purple fangs and the collar of his black cloak turned up.

DRACULA TOURS, it said. I nearly got off the plane there and then, except the Captain said we were passing over Leeds at 10,000 feet and climbing.

'That's two miles up,' said Duggie. He has got an evil grin.

'Long walk home from Leeds, love,' said George. 'Specially with your hip-bones sticking up round your ears.'

We got to Bucharest at five in the morning. The Customs man was yawning. Till he opened our suitcase. He held up the mallet and pegs at George in a very rude way.

'Vat for, pliss?'

'Camping, you great Commie nerk. We go campee, chop-chop?' He went through the motions of putting up a tent, and started to hammer one of the tent-pegs into the real marble floor (I must say these Commies do do things in style).

'The People's Republic of Rumania are renowned for their camp-equipments of the very highest standard. All will be provided . . .'

'Look, mate,' said George, holding one of the ash-stakes to within half an inch of the man's nose. 'That's British craftsmanship that is. You heard of British craftsmanship – British Leyland? Chop-chop?'

A crowd started to gather, including two men in those black leather raincoats like they have. With sneery looks on their faces like Mr Montgomery in our underwear department, whose wife left him last August and he's never got over it . . . But when George said 'British Leyland' they all walked away screwing fingers into their ears and saying 'British Leyland, British Leyland'. All except the two men in leather raincoats, who asked Duggie whether he supported Manchester United. When he said yes, they said 'Iss matter for ordinary police' and went away too.

Then our courier comes up, and winks at the Customs man and looks at George and waggles his elbow (though George has only had six Vodkas and they ought to see him when he's had ten). So the Customs man shrugs and chalks our bag. And we all go off in a really nice centrally-heated bus to the hotel at Cluj. There was a lot of snow, but I didn't see any sleighs or wolves. George said it was on account of all the Rumanians now working in tractor factories; wolves are scarce and they keep them for the tourists. But it was a bit disappointing – I mean you can see a tractor factory or a collective farm in Manchester any day, can't you?

I must say the hotel was really cosy. The courier said it had once been a Nobleman's Palace. And the marble pillars with gold tops and chandeliers which are now fully-electric made me feel like Cinderella. George said it was a long time till midnight, and Duggie said he'd buy me a pumpkin in the morning. Even the toilets were all marble and gold and so clean you could eat your breakfast off the floor. Only, the woman in charge was in uniform with black boots and I was frightened she might unlock the loo door and ask to see my passport while I was concerned with private arrangements.

And so to bed, in a four-poster fit for the Nobleman and his light-of-love. George had a bottle of duty-free Vodka and he and Duggie sat up talking till God knows when, but I had my latest Mills and Boon and, I'm proud to say, soon read myself to sleep. Oh, and I forgot to tell you, we were on the fourth floor, and there was a sheer drop to the street where the State garbage-collectors or something were moving as small as beetles.

Next evening, we were booked in for a concert given by the Garmentworkers' Collective Choir, followed by a typical Transylvanian Feast.

I quite enjoyed the choir; their costumes were traditional and they had sewn every stitch them-selves – some of the men's smocks contained 10,000 stitches! I found their songs quaint – we were given leaflets with the words in English, and *they* were even

quainter. Can you believe it – one song went 'My cow
has baked an apple pie'. I fear someone had not done
their English homework!

George and Duggie, however, behaved badly. After
the first song, George said loudly that our little cat's
boyfriends made a better noise, and what time did the
bar open? (He knew very well what time, of course –
he was only doing it to *provoke*.)

After the second song, he and Duggie walked out,
saying they were wasting good drinking-time. As we
were sitting in the front row, it was very embarrassing,
and I felt a proper fool, with an empty chair each side
of me and everybody *staring*. But a nice little man
came and sat next to me, for the rest of the concert.
Ever so sweet and attentive – great big soulful brown
eyes, and a curvy nose just like Burt Reynolds'. In
spite of his wrinkles and balding, it was quite Romantic. As you know, I have a weakness for older men . . .
anyway, he said his name was Mihaly Bocskay. He
wrote it down for me and tried to teach me to say it,
then said I could call him Michael but he didn't like
Mike. He had beautiful manners (all Rumanian men
except the policemen have) but looked very sad. I
kept wondering if he wasn't the Nobleman who'd once
owned the hotel when it was a real home. When the
concert was over, he took me in to the Feast, but we
had just sat down when George and Duggie arrived,
rather the worse for wear, I'm afraid.

'Hey up, Alfonso,' said George to Mihaly. 'D'you
mind budging up so I can sit next to my missus?'
George calls all foreigners Alfonso, though I'm sure
they don't like it. How Mihaly kept his temper I don't

know. I was expecting him to excuse himself at any moment, but he didn't.

Once George had his chicken-leg in one hand and his sparkling-type Rumanian champagne in the other, he turned quite friendly.

'Hey up, Alfonso, what you reckon to all this vampire rubbish, then?'

Mihaly smiled his sad little smile, and lifted his hands, palm upwards, the way Continentals do. 'Not nonsense, sir. Part of our way of life. Since prehistoric times, Rumanians have worshipped their dead more than the Gods. After the dead have been in the earth for three, or five, or seven years, we still exhume their bones, wrap them in clean linen and re-inter them.'

I gasped with horror. Duggie said, 'It's like Man United Supporters . . .'

'What you mean?' roared George. 'Like Man United supporters?'

'When they've been cremated, they get their wives to scatter their ashes in the goal-mouth at the Old Trafford end . . .'

'What the hell's that got to do with it?'

'Only thought I'd mention it!'

'Well, don't! Go on, Alfonso – I'm buying it.'

Mihaly went on. I know exactly what he said because I found it so hard to credit I wrote it all down straight away before I went to bed.

'We have the feast of Koljada, when all the dead go round every house in the village, in the guise of beggars.'

'Just like New Year's Eve in Scotland,' said Duggie. 'Ever been on one of those, George?'

'Shurrup!'

142

'Our problem is the *Unclean* Dead . . .'

'Your actual vampires,' said George. 'Listen to this, Duggie.'

'The Unclean Dead are spirits prematurely deprived of life and its joys. Such spirits are greedy for the good things they lost and they make attempts to return to this life – to the peril of the living. Particularly dangerous are the spirits of maidens who die before marriage. They are believed to be addicted to the kidnapping of bridegrooms and babies. Another annual feast – Semik – on the seventh Thursday after Easter, is devoted to the expulsion of these spirits, called Viles.'

'Hey up – virgins after bridegrooms – there's hope for you yet, Duggie! Go on, Alfonso, go on.'

'These are not the only Viles – there are also all people born between Christmas Day and March the twenty-first.'

Duggie turned as white as a sheet. George, poking him with his chicken-bone, gave a bellow that brought the whole traditional feast to a standstill.

'I like it, I like it. Wait till the lads at Leyland know you're a Vile, Duggie – they'll chuck you out'ut union. You'll have to join the NUV – won't he, Alfonso? And get himself a virgin bride, and have a whole football team of little vampires . . .'

'Shurrup,' said Duggie, shifting uncomfortably. Any mention of Romance makes Duggie ill-at-ease.

'I don't blame you getting fed up, Duggie, old lad – it's a vile prospect – get it, Alfonso – a *vile* prospect?'

'We are still sadly pagan,' said Mihaly. 'But with priests who lend their presence at the exhumation and destruction of vampires, what can you expect?'

'The old ash-stake, eh? Wham-wham?' Everyone was staring at us now.

'In extreme cases. The dead who will not decompose are surely vampires. Usually it is enough for relatives to light fires on the graves, or water them regularly, to hurry decomposition of the body.'

'So the bones can be dug up and given a three-year MOT sooner. Fascinating that, eh, Duggie?'

Duggie had turned green. 'Rumania's just not civilised. We should never have let them into the Common Market.'

'Not civilised?' asked Mihaly, mildly. 'In Bulgaria they bury people *alive* to cure epidemics.'

'But look, Alfonso, how do you do-in a vampire, in extreme cases, like?'

'They must always return to their graves at daybreak, or to a coffin filled with their native earth. You must exhume the corpse and burn it, or drive a stake down through the grave so it passes through the corpse's heart.'

'Like an ash-stake?'

'Any wood will do. We do not have many ash trees in Transylvania. Excuse me, I must leave you. Au revoir, Madame.'

'Nice feller that. Elevating conversation. Must be a Professor or something.'

Another Rumanian man leaned over from the next table, with a smile. 'No, he is not a Professor – he is the night-superintendent at the tram-depot.'

'Shame – see what comes of nationalisation, Duggie? In the Free West, he'd be a Professor for certain.' George always likes to have the last word.

Unfortunately, it wasn't the last word. Alfonso –

144

Mihaly I mean – had really set them off about vampires. George tried to bite Duggie on the neck, pretending to be a virgin-vampire by stuffing two oranges
into the top-pockets of his best safari-jacket. Then
they started sussing out the waitresses who were passing among us with frothing steins of beer. Which was
funny, really, because normally they only notice cars
and motorbikes, and the brewery-names on pub-signs.

A buxom rosy-cheeked serving wench, in low-cut
peasant smock, swam past in a shower of warm beer.

'Drac's certainly not been giving her a six-thou-
sand-mile road-test recently,' said George, smacking
his lips . . . And me sitting there!

'What about *that* one, though,' said Duggie, pointing rudely.

The next waitress, a large blonde lady with a lot of
lace round her throat, wasn't moving half so fast. In
fact, she looked quite wobbly and weary, sweaty and
pale.

'That's the one,' said George, grabbing her plump
shoulder and pulling at her lace collar like a Viking
on the Pillage. We all looked, and there were two
large red spots an inch apart on her milky-white
throat. Would you believe it? I felt quite swimmy
myself for a moment.

'What's those?' roared George, pointing at the red
spots.

'Pliss?'

'Well, they're not bloody Scotch mist,' shouted
George. 'Where *is* he, missus? Where is the crafty
sod? Lead me to him an' I'll bloody well crucify him.'
I think he meant it kindly, but I don't think the lady
understood. She fainted. It's lucky George was big

enough to catch her, and carry her to safety (heavy as she was) like a real hero.

I think myself he was misunderstood. There were some vinegar looks from our coach party, I can tell you. And four waiters came hurrying across, and a man in a black leather coat. George nearly vanished under the crowd. But I could hear him saying, 'What do you think these are then, Scotch mist?' over and over.

Duggie just stood with his mouth open, not looking like Robert Redford at all. Anyway, it ended with George dumping the waitress on to the five of them, and it took all five of them to carry her away. George came back dusting off his safari-jacket and saying,

'Bloody Commies and they haven't even got a National Health Service.'

I couldn't hardly sleep that night, thinking about that poor girl and what she must have been through. Was it really Dracula and what had it really been like? Worse even than my wedding-night when George stayed up till five a.m. helping Duggie with his corroded sub-frames? But I read half of *Her Healing Lover* and that sent me off in the end.

You'll never believe this, but the next morning we drove straight to Count Dracula's castle. I mean, Count Dracula was a *real* person, only he's really called Count Vlad. And he wasn't really a vampire at all, but only a cruel nobleman who impaled his enemies on stakes and left them to die a lingering death. Or so Mr Dearman the courier told us.

146

'Quite humane, really,' said Duggie, nudging George.

'A real friend to the workers,' said George.

'How do you know it was the workers he impaled?'

'Son,' said George, taking him by the shoulders, 'by the time you get to my age, you realise it's always the workers who get impaled. And up yours and all, mate,' he added, to a man in a black leather raincoat who was passing slowly above our heads, pacing the ramparts with his hands in his pockets. I was sure it was one of the two men from last night.

'Lead on to the place of impalement,' shouts George, thrusting his arm in the air. 'Or shall we start with the bathroom?'

'What bathroom?' asked Mr Dearman; 'cos the castle didn't look that sort of place.

'The *blood*-bath room,' shouts George and he and Duggie were laughing so much they nearly fell off the gatehouse. I was ever so ashamed. But they sort of quietened down by the time we got to the torture-chambers and dungeons. Well, a bit. George managed to fasten Duggie's neck into a neck-shackle and then couldn't get it undone and Mr Dearman had to fetch a man with a key, and Duggie's shirt-collar was all rusty when they got it off.

'Snap-lock,' said George, disgusted. 'The Commies are underhand bastards.' (Duggie didn't say much; he kept coughing, and his face was a funny colour all the time till we had a nice cup of coffee in the local Hall of the Proletariat afterwards.)

But that didn't stop him and George knocking on walls and rapping on locked doors, and even getting out a measuring-tape and measuring the floors.

147

'The crafty sod's got himself hidden somewhere,' said George. 'They don't fool me with all that impaling rubbish. There wouldn't be all those books and films about him, if he wasn't true. Hey, mate, where's the chapel crypt?'

'There is no crypt!' shouted Mr Dearman, who was busy answering some pretty urgent questions from the man in the black leather raincoat. 'I've *told* you, Count Dracula was a *myth*, invented by the Victorian novelist Bram Stoker. He doesn't *exist*.' There were tears in his eyes, but it might have been just the cold wind, coming across the fir trees.

'And pigs might fly,' said George. Then he turned to the man in the black coat. 'Where's the chapel crypt, mate?'

'You are *religious*?' asked the man suspiciously. Mr Dearman got him to go away in the end. George and Duggie went on tapping.

Suddenly George said, 'Secret door here, Duggie, it's loose.' He heaved at some stonework which broke off, revealing nothing but more stonework. The man in black came back and George handed him the stonework. 'Came away in me hand – bad craftsmanship, squire, typical Commie rubbish. Like Moskwitches – unsafe at any speed. Chop-chop.'

'Coffee is now available at the Hall of the Proletariat,' said the man in black, his jaws working.

'Christ, it speaks English proper,' said George.

'Might as well drink their ersatz coffee,' said Duggie. 'They make it from roasted acorns. We can't do nothing here at the moment.'

That 'at the moment' sent a real shiver up my spine. But it was a *nice* cup of coffee at the Hall of the

Proletariat – just like that mild blend you can get at Tesco's. And we had a merry time on the way back to the hotel. George took Duggie into that little toilet they have at the back of the coach, and got him up as Count Dracula himself! With a big black polythene cloak and plastic fangs, and Duggie came leaping down the gangway making all us ladies scream. Also Mr Dearman, whose foot he trod on. Duggie bit all us ladies on the neck, even the elderly ones, which I thought was nice of him. They were delighted, since, as I told you before, he is quite nice-looking, being like Robert Redford, only with a little ginger moustache. Then we sang our English songs all the way back to Cluj, and all the people we passed looked up kindly. It made it feel like home and even Mr Dearman cheered up.

That afternoon, after a full four-course lunch, we were left free to disport ourselves with activities of our own choice. I did the Old Shoe Museum and the knitwear-collective, which was quite nice, though you couldn't imagine Count Dracula having his way with many of the knitting-girls, who have very large muscles even when quite young.

George and Duggie went off on their own; Duggie wearing six pairs of jeans, which made him rather an odd shape (covered up by his duffle-coat).

'You're bloody mad,' said Duggie (you must excuse the language, but I do want to give you the whole unvarnished truth). 'You're mad. You'll never get one.'

'Listen mate,' said George (I knew from his voice he had taken Duggie by the elbow), 'Before my old man left home for good, he gave me one bit of excellent advice. He'd been all over the world, my dad, Hong Kong, Buenos Aires . . .'

'Saudi,' suggested Duggie.

'Saudi. And my old dad said to me, wherever you are in the world, in the back-streets of any town you'll find a little old garage, and in that garage will be a little old man who'll do *anything* for you, if your price is right. And those English jeans you're wearing *is* the right price, anywhere behind the Iron Curtain. You could have the Prima Ballerina of the Bolshoi Ballet for a pair of Wranglers.'

'But these aren't English jeans – they're made in Hong Kong.'

'Same difference, mate. How would these stupid buggers know?'

I must confess I left for the Old Shoe Museum in a fit of trembling. But worse was to follow. When I got back, our little bedroom was littered. Crash-helmets, a rope with a big hook on the end, and a large crowbar.

'Told you you could get anything for a pair of English jeans!'

'Three pair,' said Duggie, shivering. 'I miss them.'

'We've got a motorbike!'

'Bloody CZ 250 – it won't do fifty mile an hour, pulling that sidecar. Did you hear that piston-slap?'

'Nothing a new flint won't cure. Anyway, it's only eighty kilometres – fifty miles to you. We can be back by midnight. Once we get a straight run at that castle, undisturbed, I reckon I can put my finger on that crafty bastard in half an hour. These Commie-castles is worse put together than their cars – fall apart in your hand.'

'He won't be there. They're only in their coffins from sunrise to sunset.'

'OK, we'll suss out where he shacks up, and do him first thing tomorrow morning.'

'I demand to know where you're going,' I said, like the wife in *Rebecca*.

'Out,' said George.

'What about the Folk Dance?'

'Folk the Folk-dance,' said George, heaving on his gear. He never looked so much himself as in motor-bike-gear. Big as a house. 'Don't do anything I wouldn't do – and lay off the sodding Vodka – you know what you're like. Got the mallet, Duggie? Right. Fire-escape's at the end of the corridor.'

They vanished, and I switched on the light in a hurry. Dusk was gathering in the corners of our bedroom, rather suddenly.

I must admit I enjoyed the dinner and folk-dance. People did ask where George and Duggie were. I told them all the foreign food hadn't agreed with them, and they were indisposed. I'm afraid Mr Dearman bent his elbow and tilted an imaginary glass, rather spitefully, and a lot of ignorant people laughed. But I ignored them, like you once advised me, and it soon passed off.

Mihaly was at the dinner. He was quite the beau. Stayed with me all evening and taught me to folk-dance. The only jarring note was that he kept enquiring about George and Duggie's health. At my door, he asked could he come in for a moment, but when I blushed he said goodnight immediately. Only he was still trying to peer into the bedroom as I let myself in with my key. I think he was worried what George might think . . .

Anyway, when I looked at my watch, it was midnight and no sign of George. I should have felt worried, but thought of Mary Stewart's heroine in *Touch Not the Cat* and tried to remain pert and insouciant. I got into my see-through nightdress and negligee (not that George ever notices – I might as well wear flannelette as far as he's concerned) and sat at the rococo dressing-table, brushing my hair. (They tell me my hair is my crowning glory – it's gold and comes down as far as my waist and sparks when I brush it.) I remember thinking, 'If anything is going to happen, it will happen now.' Wasn't that a funny thought to have?

Anyway, I looked in the mirror and saw behind me the uncurtained window and mist rising, glowing in the light from my room.

But when I got up and went to the window, worrying about George, I could see right up and down the empty street, quite clear. The mist was just outside *my* window. I thought someone must have been having a bath downstairs, and running the water out.

But it went on and on. So I thought it must be the kitchen down there; only who'd want to be cooking at midnight? Or a leak in the steam-heat. The steam somehow got smaller, but thicker, and suddenly I couldn't help giving a little squeak.

There was a man standing on the ledge outside; only when I peered down I couldn't *see* any ledge. Perhaps he was hanging in one of those strap-things

152

that window-cleaners let themselves down on, like at my Gran's tower-block in Miles Platting.

'Have you come to mend the plumbing?' I shouted through the glass, because those Commie-people work at the craziest hours.

He turned and looked at me. Oh, he had a lovely face – a bit like Mihaly's but young and smooth, not worried. His eyes were that same blue as Paul Newman's. And his hair was like black silk. And he was wearing evening-dress, like he'd just come from the opera. But he wouldn't come straight from the opera to mend the plumbing, would he? I mean, I didn't know how they did things behind the Iron Curtain.

'Open the window,' he mouthed through the glass, clear as clear. He had lovely teeth, really Pepsodent-white.

'It's not convenient,' I shouted. 'I'm not decent. Go round to the fire-escape – George left it open.'

He shook his head, looking a bit vexed. I was frightened he might fall off the ledge. I mean, why be prudish when there's life at stake? So I opened the window (I had a terrible job with the double-glazing) and he came in and thanked me and kissed my hand, very Romantic. I remember thinking, one day my prince has come! I was a bit confused; all that sparkling-type Rumanian champagne, I think.

'George,' I said faintly. Not crying for help; more worried George would come back and find us and take it all wrong . . .

'Do not worry about George, Madame.' (They always call you Madame – French-like. Not like the

153

way they called you 'madam' in Debenhams.) 'Do not worry about George – he is miles away.'

'You don't know George,' I said.

'But I do know George. He has made it his business to interfere with me, so I am making it my business to interfere with him. It is thanks to George that my little friend Zsa-Zsa is lying in Cluj Hospital in intensive care, having a blood transfusion . . .'

'Is that the waitress?'

'The same, Madame. And now, permit me . . .' His eyes were glowing, lovely. Honestly, it's cruel how they depict him at the pictures . . . all mouldy fangs and that. He was the perfect gentleman from start to finish. For instance, I said, 'Let me take my nightie off. I don't want to get blood all over it – it's new. Do you like it?'

'Very much, Madame. You have exquisite taste.'

Which is more than George ever said. I don't want to discuss what happened next – it's a personal matter. Except his teeth didn't hurt at all. I didn't feel a thing – like going to old Mr Padgett, our dentist in Owley Road.

'What the hell's up wi' you?' roared George, banging the lights on. 'Get yourself decent – Duggie's here.' He was standing there in his leathers, big as a house, face all dirty and hair full of dust. Duggie was standing behind him, looking sheepish and anywhere but in my direction. I pulled on my negligee to cover my confusion.

'We didn't find nothing,' said Duggie, when his eyes came back into focus. 'George knocked down a wall and we got rumbled. Bloody night-watchmen have got *guns* in Rumania.'

'That feller couldn't hit a goldfish in a piss-pot,' said George. 'Anyway, what the hell's up wi' you?'

'Nothing,' I said. 'I just feel ... languorous.' Actually, I felt smashing. I've never felt like that before. All curled-up inside like a kitten – you know. Only I was stupid enough to put my fingers to my throat. I mean, George usually never looks at me ... but he was throat-crazy by that time.

His roar of rage brought the night-manager knocking on the door, from five floors down. And he took a lot of getting rid of. After he'd gone, George just sat there, slapping his knee with his gauntlet.

'You shouldn't ha' done it, Sheila,' said Duggie to me. 'You know George thinks the world of you. I mean, look at the way he's just fitted you wall-to-wall carpeting in every room in your house ...'

'Bugger the carpeting!' I shouted (pardon my frankness). 'It's just like George. He never even notices me, till somebody else fancies me. It was the same when it was Norman Siddall in our furniture department ...'

'I settled Norman Siddall,' said George, 'an' I'll settle this bugger an' all, *if* I can find him.'

'It always gets to this point in the horror-movies,' said Duggie helpfully. 'Dracula always goes for the hero's girl.' (Notice he didn't say 'heroine'.) 'Then the hero sends for the Professor ...'

'Where the hell would I get a Professor this time o' night?'

Duggie put his arm round George's shoulders. 'That was a great truth, George, what your old Dad

155

told you. Anywhere in the world, if you look in the back-streets you'll find a little garage with a little old man in it . . .'

'He lives over that garage,' said George, getting up and looking more cheerful. 'Fetch some more of them Hong Kong jeans, Duggie.'

The Professor was little and old and smelt of mothballs and he hugged his two pair of Hong Kong jeans to him, like they were the Crown Jewels. I knew he was little and smelly, because he was sitting on my knee in the sidecar of the cz. And I was sitting on the ash-stakes and mallet. With Duggie two-up behind George, I don't know how we climbed those hills at all.

'I don't like that piston-slap,' said Duggie.

'These bikes are like donkeys,' shouted George, as we topped another hill and the slipstream grew again. 'Not fast, but give 'em a good kick an' they'll go on forever.'

I thought how unlike a sleigh-ride it was. But that's life. Every time I buy a bit of cut-price cheese at Mono-store, there's always a bit of mould on it . . .

George had thought of leaving me behind. He'd made me lie on the bed, and sprinkled three jars of dried garlic over me, and splashed me with the water from Halford's. And chalked crosses all over the bed and the door and window and then announced he didn't trust me any more. I was still feeling a bit damp, and I did smell like an Italian waiter. Though not as bad as the Professor . . .

Anyway, there we were bucketing on through the

moonlight, past the Castle of Count Vlad the Impaler, and all the floodlights were on and men with guns prowling around looking for someone to shoot, and you could see what George had done to the wall . . .

On we went again, and it was lovely. The Carpathian Mountains, all with snow on, looking like Martini the Bright One, the Right One. And the headlamps picking up spectral trees and white owls flying over the road ever so slow.

Then we pulled up behind the V.I. Lenin Jammaking Factory. And there it all was – a little hill rising up through a lake of mist with three gaunt fir trees and a ruinous church with a little onion-dome on top and all tilting gravestones round. It looked just like the start of 'The Sideboard of Doctor Caligari', except for the jam-factory, and I held George's hand and wished I was still *his* fiancée . . .

Distant black shapes came swooping down to the ruined church, outlined against the rosy flush of dawn (I always got top marks for composition at school) and I said,

'Oh, George, look at them crows,' and he said,

'If them's crows, them trees is no bigger nor privetbushes. That's your boyfriend, Count Drac an' his little mates, coming home wi' the Express Dairy.' And my heart went thump, 'cos I wanted to see Count Drac again. But my heart was uneasy within my breast.

Anyway, George gave me a shove, and we started across the graveyard. It was hard, because there was all fallen gravestones and tangled briars under a foot of snow and we had to slither. I was still slithering when George and the Professor reached the church. (Duggie had got his ankle stuck down a grave-hole.)

157

I saw the Professor point to a slab with a ring in it, on the church floor, and George took off his crash-helmet and spat on his hands and got heaving. I could tell it was heavy, but George takes a lot of stopping once he gets started, and by the time I'd rescued Duggie's foot and we'd got there, the trapdoor was gaping and open. Such a pong – I suppose it was the native earth that they have to have in their coffins, and I don't know what vampires do about going to the toilet . . .

George spits on his hands again and says, 'It's just like eating an' fighting, Duggie – it's all a matter of getting started. Where's the mallet?' And for once, Duggie had what was needed, which was more than he had on our wedding-day, when my Dad had to drive him home in the car to fetch the ring.

Down we go, and there was all coffins lying about any old how, some slimy, some not, like when my Aunty Doreen was moved by Pickford's . . . I realised it was all real, like the Hammer House of Horrors, and my heart missed a beat. Was I truly to see my lovely Count Dracula again?

George heaved up a coffin-lid and said 'Sorry, Missus' in an embarrassed way (just like when he went to mend Mr Sampson's lav-window and Mrs Sampson was sitting there). For indeed there was a lovely girl inside the coffin, her shapely limbs clad only in a thin diaphanous nightgown.

'Hey, Duggie, here's your virgin-vampire, looking for a bridegroom. Your luck's in.'

The lady opened her big blue eyes and hissed at George, like our little pussy does when he accidentally treads on her tail. She sort of tried to claw him with blood-red talons, but she couldn't quite reach, and she opened her ripe lips in a snarl, showing long fangs like they always do.

'Well,' said George, 'I'll vouch for the vampire, but I'm not so sure about the virgin. Hey, she's getting impatient, Duggie, to feel your hot lustful hands on her maidenly flesh . . .'

'Shurrup,' said Duggie, shuffling his feet. Women always made him embarrassed.

'Sorry, Missus, must get cracking,' said George, slamming the lid down on her. 'I've got a big stake in this business. Did you get that, Duggie, eh? I got a big *stake* in this business. You haven't forgotten the stakes Duggie, by any chance?'

'No,' said Duggie. 'Shurrup.' I could tell he was still embarrassed about the young lady in the diaphanous nightdress. His mother brought him up nice; I'll say that for her.

George ran to and fro across the ghastly crypt, banging on the coffins left right and centre, singing 'Don't go lurking at the back, Drac.' Then he came to a coffin so old and huge and gilded and cobwebby and pongy that it had to be . . .

'Der-deeeeeerrr!' boomed George, flipping back the lid like he was Tommy Cooper. And there was my beautiful Count, lying quite calmly with his elegantly manicured hands folded across his frilly evening-shirt, and smiling up at George his little smile.

'You can take that look off your face,' shouts George. 'Norman Siddall was laughing till I hit him . . .'

The Count went on smiling. He did have lovely eyes.

159

'Stake,' said George, holding out his hand. 'Mallet.' Doing his hospital-act, like Hawkeye in MASH. He put the point of the stake on Count Dracula's chest, and got a good grip on the mallet.

'Are you sure his heart's on that side?' asks Duggie snidely. 'I was always taught at school it was on the left.'

'Education's sodding wonderful,' says George, shifting the stake. 'I always said Dracula's heart was in the right place.'

'Where it will remain,' said a cool voice behind us. The light from the trap-door darkened. And there was Michael Bocskay coming down the steps, with two other men in black leather raincoats and five with grey uniforms and red stars in their fur caps and them sub-machine-guns, all pointing at George's best leather jacket.

'Hell,' said George. 'It's Alfonso! Come to see the fun?'

'There will be no fun. I will take the mallet. You are under arrest.'

'On what charge?' shouted George, quite heroically, considering. 'We're doing Christian work here!'

Michael flipped his notebook open. 'Bribing a State official. Driving without a State driving-licence. Driving without a current insurance. Driving without road-fund tax. Driving with unroadworthy tyres. Castle-breaking and entering. Need I go on?'

'I'll bloody kill you,' George roared at the cowering Professor. 'You said that bike was taxed and insured.' He threw the Professor at the two men in black leather. Who caught him, and rapidly relieved him of the Hong Kong jeans he was still clutching.

'You could spend ten years in our jails,' said Michael. 'Besides the greater charge of sabotage against the Rumanian People's Republic.'

'Sabotage – finishing off that crafty slinking bastard?'

'Sabotage. Why did you come to Transylvania? To inspect our jam and knitwear factories? To enjoy the singing of the Garmentworkers' Choir?'

'To find Dracula.'

'And so will many thousand others. Dracula lives, my stupid friend, and will continue to do so, while I am his State security-officer.'

'I thought you were the night-cleaning superintendent at the tram-depot?'

'Each man in his time plays many parts,' said Michael, with a flourish.

'What's the alternative?' asked George craftily. He knew his policemen, did George; the world over.

'The alternative is three weeks luxury-sunbathing holiday at the glorious Black Sea resort of Varna in Bulgaria.'

'Where they bury people alive to stop epidemics?'

'There are no epidemics in Varna. It has the best health-figures for any town in the Cominform.'

'Done,' said George.

So here I am, painting my toe-nails in the Solarium (that's sun-room to you) of the Oktober Revolution State Sanatorium in Varna. Staring out at the Black Sea. George is outside with Duggie, on the Prom. They are trying to help a man start his car. But that was half an hour ago, and now a crowd is gathering.

161

George is making his eternal speech that Russian cars are crap, but Duggie is looking nervously at a man in a black leather coat on the fringes of the crowd.

And I miss my dear Count Dracula. Oh, Aunty Evelyn, what shall I do? Stay here among the fat Russian women, being ogled by the Russian men because I am the only female here under nine stone? Shall I go back this weekend to 24 Smith Terrace and our little cat and Sunday tea with Mum? Or shall I nick all George's traveller's cheques and take the bus back to Cluj, and walk out into the snow hoping my Count Dracula will find me before I freeze to death? I somehow know he will sense my coming and fly to meet me, before George has even realised I've gone. And I shall lie in an ancient coffin, my limbs clad only in a diaphanous nightgown . . .

What would you do, dear Aunty Evelyn?

A Walk on the Wild Side

To live with a cat is to live with fear.

You can keep dogs safe till they die of obesity; collar-and-lead and walkies-in-the-park. But not cats; cats like a walk on the wild side.

You *can* deny cat-nature. Like the childless couple down our lane, whose white Persians never leave the house except in spotless white cages for their monthly trip to the vet. Those cats sit endlessly in their upstairs bedroom window, staring out at the moving world, sometimes raising a futile paw to the glass. But mostly, they're still; for a while, I thought they were stuffed toys.

Everything should be allowed to live and die, according to its nature. But cats have two natures. Take my tortoiseshell, Melly. Indoors, she's a fawner, on to my knee the moment I sit down, purring, drooling, craving my approving hand. A harmless suppliant . . .

My neighbours call her the bird-catcher. She hunts their garden, filling their empty, pensioned lives with displays of predatory cunning better than TV safaris into Africa.

She's a diplomat; never brings a bird home.

I've seen her myself, late at night, crossing the

backyards of our lane like an Olympic hurdler, under sparse orange street-lamps. I've called, but she ignored me, passing overhead without a break in her stride. On the wild side.

Two natures. A purring bundle in your arms; a contemplative Buddha by the fire. But those pointed ears are moving even in sleep, listening to the windy dark outside. Suddenly, though you've heard nothing, they're on their feet, away with a thunderous rattle through the cat-flap. Sometimes they're back in your lap within five minutes; sometimes they're returned next morning (by a neighbour who can't look you in the face), a stiff-legged sodden corpse in a plastic carrier-bag. You never get a chance to say goodbye. But everything according to its nature ...

I used to enjoy a walk on the wild side. Even into my forties, the fire only had to burn blue on a winter's night, and I was out walking under the frosty stars. But now my legs ache after a day at school, the blue-burning coals just make me fetch a whisky and snuggle deeper into my book. My cats walk the wild side for me, coming home with a hint of rain on their fur, or spears of cold, or the smell of benzine from the old chemical works. When I bury my face in their coat, I know what the world's doing outside.

Like the Three Kings, they bear gifts. Live worms, that I return instantly to the nearest patch of earth. Tattered moths, beyond saving, transformed from fun to food in one scrunch. Once my old tom, Ginger, taunted because he couldn't hunt like the girls, returned with that mournful yowl of success, and a packet of fresh bacon in his mouth. I fried it for supper, gave him his tithe.

But the oddest thing Ginger brought home, on a Hallowe'en of intense frost, was a tiny live kitten, exactly the same colour as himself. That was the only reason we didn't think it was a rat, for its ears were still flat to its skull, its eyes unopened, and it was soaking from his mouth.

We shouted ridiculous things at him, demanding to know where he got it, insisting he take it back to its mother. He blinked his ridicule and left the house, implying he'd done his bit, and it was now up to us.

My wife was a loving soul. She didn't love cats much; just all living things, and cats for my sake. Our hearthrug became an instant hospital of tumbled blankets and screwed-up towels, warm milk and eye-droppers. She took over the fiddly business of six feeds a day.

Typically, the young female (for she was female, though ginger) repaid her efforts by becoming entirely devoted to me. From the beginning, she slept contented on my shoulder while I read. By four weeks, she would slowly and agonisingly climb my legs to get there.

I called her Rama, for no particular reason. My wife said it sounded like a brand of furniture-polish. For all her poor beginning, Rama grew amazingly fast. At Christmas, in a fit of childish glee, we gave each of our cats a lump of chicken. There was a sudden spat, and when we looked again, Rama had one piece under each paw, and one in her mouth. Young as she was, none of the others tried a challenge. That night, Ginger left home for good, and took up residence at the village launderette.

Then came the battle for my lap, which any male

owner of she-cats knows. The others would often lie side by side, apparently peaceful, but occasionally stretching and trying to push each other off. Or they'd deliberately lie on top of each other, making me part of a cat-sandwich. They'd even come to blows between my legs, which is worrying if not downright agonising.

Rama had no truck with that sort of thing. The moment she entered the room, she'd give one *look*, and the occupant of my knee would instantly depart.

She had the same effortless dominance at meal-times. Four cats jostling at one saucer, and Rama eating lazily from the other. And they'd never dare *sniff* her leavings, even after she'd left the room.

And still she grew. Bigger even than old Melly, who was big for a cat. Every morning, as I brushed my hair before school, I would watch a little comedy. Rama would sit by our front gate, willing to receive all the world. And most passers-by would come across to stroke her, for she was very beautiful with her long swirling red fur, and plumed tail. But as they drew near, and saw her great size, and felt her confidence, they would grow . . . unsure. They would hover, hands half out, and then they would go away again, leaving her unstroked.

When she lay on me she began to be oppressive. Her weight was just tolerable on my aching legs, but when, consumed by some catty passion, she insisted on lying on my chest with her paws round my neck, I had to strain to breathe. And she had this habit of staring into my face at a distance of two inches. No other cat ever did that, because for cats, eye-to-eye is a challenge. But it was me that turned my eyes away;

Rama had a heavy soul, as she had a heavy body.

But her delicacy made her bearable. The others have left my thighs, my shoulders and my back a mass of tiny red scratches, with their ill-timed leaps, frantic landings and convulsive sleepy stretchings. I scarcely dare bathe, because people pass remarks that embarrass my wife. But Rama never put a claw into me, save once. She was a lovely cat to doze with. After a cold hard day at school, I tend to fall asleep over the roaring fire and the six o'clock news. With Rama on my knee, I dreamt pleasant dreams I could never remember, and woke without a stiff neck, set up for the evening.

Then she began to haunt our bedroom at bedtime. Here, my wife drew the line. Rama was carried swiftly downstairs and put out. She never struggled, but there was a laying-back of ears that left her opinion in no doubt. Then she discovered my wife's reluctance to get up again, once warmly tucked in. So she would conceal herself early, behind the drawn bedroom curtains, or almost unbreathing in the moonlit shadow of the rubber-plant. Sometimes, as I undressed, I'd spot her hiding-place, but that great cool green eye would swear me to silence. Then, at my wife's first snore, Rama would ghost across the carpet and purr softly up into my arms.

Then she tried to go too far; and lie between my wife and me in bed. That was enough to get my wife up again, and out Rama would go.

There, for some time, the battle-line stayed drawn . . .

*

167

My son Peter, too, has always lived by his nature. A PhD in zoology, then the wardenship of a famous but utterly remote Scottish bird-reserve. A wife not only beautiful, but also zoological, and inured to their kind of genteel poverty. Happy with a three-bedroomed cottage, a chemical loo and the use of the firm's Land Rover.

Usually they manage things so that their babies are born in late July, when we can go up to Scotland and hold the fort. My wife copes with the children. I clumsily take Sheila's place, putting plastic rings on ducks, cleaning oiled cormorants, stopping elderly ornithologists falling over cliffs and being bossed around by Peter. My son is always at his most touching when about to become a father. For a few days he stops being a totally competent thirty-year-old, and runs his fingers through his hair like a baffled teenager, his thin wrists sticking miles out of the sleeves of his well-darned jumper.

But this year, for all their PhDs, they'd mistimed things. The baby was due in November. My wife drove herself up. There were snow-warnings out, and I was quite frantic until I got her call from the reserve. Then I felt sorry for myself. Our house is large, Victorian, rather isolated on the crest of the hill above the old chemical works. In fact, the old manager's house. I'd got myself a mansion on the cheap, because the view of the works halved the price, though there's a splendid view of the Frodsham Hills beyond.

Our social life is usually too busy for my taste, on top of parents' evenings and all that nonsense without which the modern parent does not think her child is being educated. But now I learnt that it was purely my

168

wife's creation; you can't hold dinner-parties without cooking. And I dislike going to the cinema on my own. In fact, I discovered that after thirty years of marriage, I disliked going *anywhere* on my own. I got pretty lonely, but I was too tired with the end of term to do anything about it.

I noticed the wind for the first time; the way the Virginia creeper tapped on the windows. My wife's presence had always abolished such things. I wasn't *scared*. More like a primitive man, exploring after dark a cave that had always been a bit too big for him, and is now much too big. My eyes noticed new shadows in the hall; my ears twitched too often as I ate my lukewarm baked beans in the big cold kitchen.

The cats were a solace. With Rama on my knee, and the others perched on chairback and mantelpiece, we were famously snug. But only Rama came to bed with me. When I wakened in the night (which I never normally do) it was good to feel her weight on the bed, and to reach out and feel her large soft furry flank rising and falling.

So I was all the more annoyed, one windy night, to be awakened at three by her insistently scratching at the door, demanding to be let out. You didn't leave Rama scratching long, if you valued your paintwork.

'Go on, then, damn you.' She vanished like a ghost along the hall, and I went back to a cold bed, feeling thoroughly deserted.

I had just dozed off when the screaming started.

Now as a Head, I consider myself an expert on the female scream, hysterical, expectant or distressed. I really can tell from a scream outside our house whether a young woman is merely drunk, or quarrelling with another female, or being sexually assaulted, enjoyably or otherwise. In fact, by sallying forth, I have prevented at least two rapes, for the area of dirty grass and trees round the old works seems to attract far more couples than our pleasant municipal park.

But this was a man screaming; in such terror as I'd not heard since my army days. Inside my house. Downstairs.

I leapt out of bed, shaking from head to foot; my pyjamas had a distressing tendency to fall down. The screaming went on and on. A door slammed. Other voices shouting. Breaking crockery.

I dialled 999 on the bedside extension, and was glad to hear the policeman's voice. When I hung up, I felt braver, especially as silence had fallen. I went to Peter's old bedroom and got his .22 rifle, remembering the good times we'd had with it, harming nothing more than empty bottles, floating in the old chemical sump. I found his box of cartridges and loaded with trembling fingers. Then, against my policeman's advice I went downstairs, switching on every light as I passed.

The kitchen was appalling; chairs tossed over, a sea of broken crockery scrunching underfoot, the back door swinging. Splashes of red among the broken saucers. I thought someone had broken my bottle of tomato ketchup, but when I tasted it, it was blood.

Oh, my poor cats . . . they live in the kitchen at night.

But when I looked around, there they were, Melly and Tiddy and Vicky and Dunnings, perched high on the Welsh dresser, crouching under the gas stove, saucer-eyed, paralysed with terror, but otherwise unharmed. All except Rama, my poor Rama, who had tried to warn me only ten minutes before.

A policeman came in through the swinging back door, the radio clipped to his tunic prattling.

'You the householder, sir?'

'I phoned you, yes.'

He looked round. 'Burglary or domestic quarrel?'

I wondered how some people must live, then said shortly, 'My wife's away in Scotland. I'm alone in the house.'

'Better put that gun down, sir. Is it loaded?'

I put the safety-catch on. 'I have a licence,' I said, wondering how out of date it was.

Another policeman appeared, dangled his hand knowingly through a circular hole in the glass of the back door. 'Burglary – pro job. There's a thirty-hundredweight van parked down the back lane. Liverpool registration – some punter called Moore – they're sussing him out on the crime-computer now.'

'Some burglary – you seen *that*?' The first copper indicated a gout of blood with his shiny toecap. 'You're not injured, sir?' They surveyed my sagging pyjamas.

'No, no!'

Their eyes went as hard as marbles. 'You shot someone, sir? In the course of preventing the burglary?'

'No, no. Smell the gun – it's not been fired.' They smelled it, looked even more baffled.

'I'm afraid they may have killed one of my cats,' I said. It was absurdly hard not to cry.

They noticed the cats for the first time; poked their rigid bodies.

'One missing, sir? Lot of blood for a cat . . .'

'They've left a nice set of dabs.' The second police-man pointed to the wall behind the open back door.

On it was a complete print of a human hand, made in what appeared to be blood.

I wearily picked up the last fragment of crockery, and put it in the waste-bin. Ran some water into a bucket and began to wash the floor. The forensic experts had taken till lunchtime, made the mess a hell of a sight worse. I wasn't going to make it to school that day. I'd just rung my secretary when the doorbell rang.

White raincoat, trilby hat. Sergeant Watkinson, CID.

'You'll be pleased to hear we picked up one of the gang, sir. *And* we got the names of the rest. He told us everything we wanted to know – when he came out from the anaesthetic.'

'Anaesthetic?'

'We picked him up at Liverpool City Hospital. They'd dumped him there – couldn't cope. He's lost an eye.'

'An eye?' I said stupidly. He changed tack, keeping me guessing.

'They're a known gang, specialising in antiques. Come round the houses, asking if you've got any antiques to sell; then they break in and take them anyway, a week later. A nasty lot. I'm glad you didn't . . . encounter them sir.'

'But what *happened*?'

'I believe you keep cats, sir?' He had a . . . hunting look on his face.

I nodded towards my still-shaken brood, still huddled around the kitchen. He reached out and stroked them tentatively, one by one. 'Not very big, are they sir, ... as domestic cats go? I mean, they *look* harmless enough. This cat that was missing ... it hasn't returned, has it? How big was that one?'

'Just a big domestic cat ... what are you getting at, sergeant?'

'Well – that bloke we caught – he reckoned he got mauled by something big in the dark. You don't keep exotic cats, do you sir? A leopard or a cheetah? Very popular they're getting, with folk who can afford them.'

'Nothing like that. Just a large domestic cat. Of course, we do get tom-cats visiting through the cat-flap. A wild tom, cornered in a strange house, can be very nasty.'

'Yeah.' He didn't sound convinced. 'That bloody handprint we found on the wall, sir – doesn't corre-spond to any named member of the gang – a woman's print they think – long fingernails.' He looked at me expectantly.

'I'm afraid I can't help you, sergeant. My wife keeps her fingernails short.'

'Where's your wife staying, sir – at the moment?'

I gave him my son's phone number. 'Can I wash that handprint off the wall now?'

'You can try, sir. Try a bit of biological detergent. Blood's hard to shift.'

'Anything else?'

'Give me a ring if that other cat shows up, sir. I'd like to see it.' He paused, one hand on the open front door. 'I don't see why that villain should lie, sir – he wasn't in any fit state to lie.'

*

'Cup of tea, sergeant?'

'If you're making one, sir.' It was the third time he'd come back in search of Rama. Without success. After a week, she was still missing. But something kept drawing him to our house. CID, too, must live by their own nature.

'Your case is all sewn up,' he said, spooning in two sugars. 'We picked up the last lad yesterday, and he admitted twenty-five other break-ins. Pushover. All the stuffing knocked out of him – like all the rest. We've recovered a fair bit of stolen property . . .' He stirred his tea again, needlessly. 'They were a hard lot. If you'd gone downstairs that night, they'd have put the boot in, left you for dead. So you ought to be grateful to whatever was in your kitchen . . .'

Again, he left the question hanging in the air.

'Look, sergeant, I've never kept a leopard or jaguar. How could I, without half the town knowing? I'm a public figure. Can't afford funny business.'

'I know sir. We've made enquiries. Very solid gentleman you are, Mr Howard Snowdon. Member of Rotary . . . well-liked, too. A bit over-fond of pussies, but quite *ordinary* pussies.'

'You be careful, sergeant, or I'll start making enquiries about *you.*'

'About me, sir?'

'Your inspector is one of my old boys – so are three of your subordinates. Headmasters have their powers too, you know.'

He grinned; I grinned. He'd been good company the last week. Which had been lonelier than ever in Rama's absence.

He stood up, shook hands. 'Well, you've seen the

last of me, sir. Case all sewn up. Except I don't know what I dare put in my official report . . . that would stand up in court. I don't like loose ends . . .'

I saw him to the gate in the dusk, waited while he started his car, waved as he drove off. Turned.

Rama was sitting on the doorstep, the light of the hall behind her. At least, a silhouetted cat sat there; a very big cat indeed.

I didn't walk directly to the front door; followed the curve of the drive, because the lawn was wet, and I was only in my carpet-slippers.

If it wasn't Rama, it would run away as I approached.

If it didn't run away, it must be Rama.

The cat watched me silently, only turning its head slightly as I walked round the curve. Surely it was the light behind her that made her seem so big?

Three yards away, I faltered. Suppose it didn't run away, and it wasn't Rama?

'Rama? Rama?'

No response. There was a gardening-fork, stuck in the earth of the rose-bed, where I'd been turning-over after pruning. Slowly, I reached out my hand. I felt much better, holding the fork.

Still the cat neither moved nor spoke.

This would never do; outfaced by a bloody alley-cat? I advanced, thrusting the tines of the fork before me.

Immediately the cat stood up, stretched fore-and-aft luxuriously. Its plumed tail shot up in greeting, tip tilted slightly left. *Prook* of greeting.

Rama; almost as if she was laughing at me. I picked her up bodily and carried her in. She felt bigger;

her up bodily and carried her in. She felt bigger; several pounds heavier. Living wild, eating fresh bloody protein. Plenty of rats in the old works; even rabbits, now it's been shut for years and the grass is growing between the cobbles.

She kneaded her paws against my chest ecstatically, extruding and withdrawing her claws. I felt them, I can tell you, right through my thick pullover. I told her to lay off, but she wouldn't. I grabbed the worst-offending paw, felt the heavy bones expanding and contracting; quite beyond my power to keep them still. It was a relief to dump her on the kitchen table.

'Where've you been, you bad girl? You've had me worried sick.'

Then I realised she hadn't really; all through her absence, the other cats hadn't dared touch her food in the second saucer, or lie on my lap. They'd known she was coming back, and so, subconsciously, had I.

She extended one forepaw along the tabletop. Splayed out, a cat's paw looks like a knuckled human hand in a velvety glove, with claws where human fingernails should be. She licked between her fingers, cleaning. I looked for signs of blood, human blood.

Her paws were spotless; but then they always were.

I sat watching her eating. Recently, I'd taken to drawing the kitchen curtains at dusk, because my back garden is full of conifers as tall as a man, and when the wind got into them, they moved in a way that worried the corner of my eye. The wind was moving them tonight. There was even a white plastic bag caught in one, that might have been an idiot face. But I knew it was only a bag, because Rama was sitting on my table eating. Her eye caught its movement for

176

a moment, fascinated, then she dismissed it with a slight splaying of the ears, and returned to her plate.

I thought of phoning Sergeant Watkinson; but what was there for him to see? I much preferred Rama's company to Sergeant Watkinson's. Having finished eating, she set to, dragging one damp paw over her ear. Even the prospect of rain seemed cosy. She would sleep in my bed tonight, while the rain battered my windows.

And if she asked to go downstairs urgently?

She was doing no more than a good watchdog. OK, the burglar had lost an eye. A Doberman Pinscher would have torn his throat out. If watchdogs, why not watch-cats?

Rama stopped washing, and looked at me. In the dim kitchen, her pupils were dilated, round, like a woman's when she makes love. When that barrier of inhuman eye-slits is removed, you can share souls with a cat, as well as with any human.

Rama loved me.

Still, I would show her who owned whom. I got down Ginger's old collar, from the nail over the sink-unit. (That was the one thing the couple at the launderette hadn't stolen; they'd had great pleasure returning it to me.) I wondered how Rama would take to a collar, as I fastened it with difficulty round her muscular neck. Some cats like them, some don't.

Rama seemed almost *too* pleased; rubbing her cheekbones against the knuckles of my hand with great affection.

It occurred to me the next evening that I must change

the note inside her little collar-capsule. After all, she was called Rama, not Ginger, and as a headmaster, I value accuracy. I reached over to her, and took the paper out. To my surprise, it was not the official piece supplied by the pet-shop, but a roughly-torn scrap, brown with age. On it was scrawled, in old-fashioned indelible pencil:

I LUV U.

That was a phrase of my wife's; a standing joke between us. Whenever she left me a note on the kitchen table, asking me to turn on the oven, or get in the washing, she ended it that way. A taunt to my headmasterly prissiness, I suppose.

But this was certainly not my wife's writing. An illiterate hand, yet forceful; the pencil had torn the paper in two places.

I turned the paper over. It carried the printed heading 'British Railways'. Not 'British Rail' which is the modern version. It seemed to be part of a time-sheet, for men doing shiftwork. Dates and times had been filled in with the same indelible pencil, but in the neat printing of some railway employee, no doubt. There was nothing more; the torn-off piece was, of necessity, very small to fit inside the capsule. As a last thought, I smelt it. Damp and mould and the faint whiff of benzine. It had come from the chemical works, I had no doubt.

Who on earth could have written it?

I had a strong suspicion it might be one of my own pupils. For the most puerile joke played on a Head is better than the best joke played on anybody else. Some of my colleagues have their phones ex-directory for that very reason. I didn't bother. I got on pretty well with my lot. Caned them seldom. Some even say hello to me in the street. When I first came, they called me 'The Abominable Snowdon', but over the years it's softened to 'Old Abby'.

Good joke to catch my cat, put a new message in her collar. But why not something spicier, like 'Old Abby's a poofter'? None of them would dare write 'I luv u' in front of his mates. A lone child, a lonely child? How would he know how my wife spelt it? and that writing was . . . odd, very odd. Someone trying to disguise his fist?

I put the note carefully inside our bone-dry spare teapot. Pity Watkinson couldn't test it for prints. But we don't carry fingerprint-records of pupils, yet. Anyway, the surest way of encouraging this kind of nonsense is to take any notice of it.

I put a new name and address in Rama's collar; hoping that if they caught her again, they'd keep their tricks to the same semi-civilised level. There were a lot of water-filled shafts in that works they could've thrown her down . . .

But I refused to keep her in; she must live according to her nature.

Then I carried her up to bed. She clung to me with flattering urgency.

It was nearly bedtime, the following night, before I gave way to my impulse to look inside the name-capsule again.

Again, the name and address were gone. Another brown scrap in its place. I placed it edge-to-edge with

179

the first; they fitted exactly, torn from the same sheet. Same indelible pencil; same jagged savage writing.

KUM UP N C ME.

Another of my wife's phrases. Used when she has a mild dose of 'flu and has retired to bed before I return home. Those notes I *never* leave lying around. In our younger days, they led to some wild and joyous occasions and I would still be embarrassed if Mrs Raven, our charlady, was to find one and ask what it was.

Who on earth could have got their hands on *that* phrase? It was uncanny, almost as if my wife were hiding somewhere in the house, playing games on me.

Except for the savagery of the writing.

Just then, as if to confirm her absence, my wife rang up to tell me I was a grandfather again. A bouncing boy (why do they always bounce?) weighing seven pounds. Howard Anthony George. That pleased me; two of the names are mine. But I did warn Peter, when he came on the line, that the initials spelt 'HAG' and did he want his son to be lumbered? We settled for 'H.G.A.' in the end, which has a dignified cadence.

When I put the phone down, I felt much better. I placed both the evil-smelling notes into the teapot, and wrote out my name and address for the third time.

'What's it all about, Rama?'

She gave a short deep purr, and splayed her ears in a non-committal way that made me laugh.

I carried her up to bed again.

*

The third quarter of the time-sheet – the part with the signature. 'S. Ballard, Chief Signalman'. So, I knew where the sheet had come from. There had been railway-sidings on the far side of the chemical works. There would be a signal-box, where the points were worked from. I thought I knew where it stood. Rama had just come back from it, smelling of must and damp and benzine . . .

But why should I trail up there, in the wind and dark? That'd make the little monkeys laugh. Be all over the school in no time, rocking the discipline-boat. Still (I looked at my watch) it was gone eleven; all the little darlings should be tucked up in bed by this time, or at least stuck in front of the midnight movie.

Might as well stroll across and see what they'd been up to. Make sure it was nothing dangerous. I took down my old reefer-jacket off the kitchen door, got the lantern with the flashing red dome from the garage, made sure I had my door-key and set off. I'd left Rama eating a plate of cold fat pork, to the intense envy of the others. I think I had some idea of keeping her at home out of harm's way. But before I'd gone twenty yards, I heard the cat-flap bang behind me, and felt her weight streak past me in the dark.

And I was glad of her company, walking through the works. God, it's an awful place. The old company had no money left to run it, and the local council had no money left to demolish it. The children haunt the works, walking along the narrow overhead pipes, climbing the rusted conveyors and high girders. The most dangerous parts have been screened off by chain-link, but the children beat the chain-link flat and go on with their deadly games. Graffiti everywhere, mingled with the old industrial notices, under the wavering beam of my lantern.

NO 5 HOIST MUFC RULE OK?

DANGER CAUSTIC SODA BAZZER AND JEFF AND BILLY

We keep getting up petitions about it, and writing to our MP, but we're wasting our time. Even St George couldn't slay the dragon called No Money.

A bit of a moon broke through the clouds. The wind banged loose bits of corrugated iron, high up among the girders. My boot-soles scrunched on the poisonous cinders. Dry dead leaves from God-knows-where, trapped like people in a disaster, scurried from place to place. I thought, if I have an accident here, it'll be days before they find me.

But the moon and my lantern saw me through, with a couple of frights, and I came out on to the open plain of the sidings. Picked my way across the moon-lit empty rails to where I thought the signalbox was.

But it wasn't. It was only some little platelayers' hut with stumpy chimney. The roof had fallen, and boys had lit a fire against the outside wall.

LFC RULES. JACK BERRY'S A SLIMER

Inside, a mass of black soot and glinting shards of glass. Nothing had happened there for a very long time.

I was retracing my steps, feeling flat and foolish, when I saw a pale cat that could only have been Rama hurtling across the rails ahead of me. Following her with my eye, I at once saw the real signal-box, standing in the black shadow of the limestone-kiln. Rama streaked up the outside stair, and vanished inside. I hurried across, worried.

182

The flat roof was intact, though most of the small-paned windows had been broken, making it hard to see inside the shadowy interior. I clumped up the outside stair, unnecessarily loudly, as if to warn someone I was coming, and pushed the door. It yielded enough to let a cat in, then resisted with a metallic clink. Shining my lantern, I saw a heavy chain and rusted padlock. Giving a grunt of exasperation, I was turning to descend when I thought I heard my name called from behind the door.

'Howard?'

It must have been the wind, which was getting up. Good heavens, it was nearly midnight . . .

I'd descended two more stairs when the voice came again.

'Howard?' If you insist I describe that voice, I would say it was a woman's, low, hoarse and . . . unpractised. Like a rusty gate creaking. But I didn't want to believe it was a voice, in that awful place. *Surely*, a trick of the wind?

While I was standing hovering, like a ninny, it came a third time, unmistakable.

'Howard, I love you.'

I wanted to run; but that works was no place to run through at night. So I went back and pushed the door angrily, so that the chain rattled. Called in my headmaster's voice, that sounded so hollow in the windy silence,

'Who's there? What's going on? Open the door!'

'Howard, I love you. Howard!'

'What are you doing with my cat? If this nonsense doesn't stop immediately, I shall fetch the police.'

183

There might have been a sigh at my stupidity; or it might have been the wind.

'Howard, help me. Fetch clothes. I'm so *cold*.'

'Let go of my cat, or I will fetch the police.'

'Howard . . .' A yearning voice, a voice of endearment.

I ran down the steps, half in rage and half in terror. From a safe distance I stared up at the great broken multi-paned signal-box window. Tricky, because blowing moonlit clouds were reflecting in the glass. But I could have sworn I saw a tall shape walking, among the signal-box levers.

'Let my cat go,' I bawled, 'or I'll fetch the police.'

Silence. I ran back up the steps, almost sobbing, and tried to kick the door in. There was a flash at my feet, then Rama was past me, and streaking across the tracks for home.

Well, I had saved my friend, and that was all that mattered. I followed her at top speed, and was never so glad to be through my own front door and switching on every light in the house. I made myself a hot whisky and lemon and sat drinking it till my shivering stopped. I was still shivering and drinking when the cat-flap banged (not doing my nerves any good) and Rama came in quite cool and sat on the table washing inside her hindlegs. She gave me a couple of hard stares, as if to say 'What's all the fuss about?' Then indicated it was time for bed.

Even with her beside me, it was a long time before I slept.

*

Next afternoon, straight after school, I drove to the signal-box, to inspect it by the last glimmerings of December daylight. Solid brick, with a concrete-slab roof. Many broken panes, but the wooden window-frames intact. Nothing bigger than a cat could have wriggled through. The only way in was through the upstairs door. Laughing at my stupid fancies of the night before, I climbed the stair and rattled the chain. The lock was rusted solid; it would take an hour's work with a hacksaw . . .

'Howard?'

It shocked me more in daylight. God how it shocked me. Cars were passing on the distant main road across the sidings, their headlights casting pools of sanity. But also reminding me it was getting dark again.

'Howard, *please*. I need clothes. I'm so *cold* . . .'

'Who are you? How do you know my name?'

'Howard, bring clothes . . . I need clothes.'

'How did you get in there? What d'you want clothes *for*?'

'Because I am *naked*, Howard. See!'

I put my eye to the crack of the door. Saw rough floorboards, the rusting levers sticking up at all angles, the broken glass.

Then an eye swam out of the gloom, opposite mine. An eye I knew, yet somehow couldn't place.

'If you don't bring clothes, I shall come to you naked, Howard.'

I ran all the way back to my car.

I was tempted to sleep elsewhere that night. But when headmasters start staying in hotels in our town . . .

185

I locked the doors and snibbed the windows. Drew the curtains. Told myself to be sensible. But it's less easy to be sensible after dark, especially alone. The wind's an enemy of commonsense, and the Virginia creeper tapping, and the idiot face in the back garden . . .

My wife rang up, full of good news about mother and baby. For once, I couldn't be bothered with her. Her cheerfulness irritated, like a bluebottle buzzing against a window. I got rid of her as quickly as possible, cooked an early supper and quite failed to eat it. Finally I scraped it into the dish for the cats.

Only to discover there wasn't a cat in the kitchen. Odd! When you keep five cats there's always a couple loafing around, ear cocked for the sound of a dish being scraped.

I suddenly felt immensely lonely; damned them for their ingratitude. Then steeled myself to open the back door and call them.

The wind snatched away my voice; none of them answered. The wild bushes tossed their heads at me. The dead leaves in the yard scurried around like the trapped crowd in a burning theatre. The sound of dead leaves is the deadest sound in the world; they sound the same at night in Pompeii.

I stepped out angrily to snatch the bobbing idiot head bag from its bough. Lost my nerve halfway, ran back inside and bolted the door. For a moment it shut out the noise of wind and leaves and I heard, through the slightly-open laundry door, the sound of a cat coughing. The sickening way they cough when they crouch flat to the ground and stick their necks out, so long you think they're choking to death.

A sign of fear in a cat. I followed the noise. The laundry seemed empty. The arrangement of washing-machine and blue plastic bowl, that I'd left myself the day before, seemed to sneer at me. I was just putting the light out, thinking I'd been imagining things, when the low desperate coughing started again.

There was a deep, dark narrow gap between the cupboard and the wall. I thrust my hand in and felt, at the back, a wire-tense bundle of fur, which I dragged out by the scruff. She fought all the way, digging in her claws and ripping the lino. Melly. For a second she lay still in my arms, eyes screwed tight-shut, ears back. Then she exploded back into the narrow gap like a furry missile, knocking over a chair that stood in her way. Leaving me with a torn shirt and bleeding arms.

I left her; I know terror when I see it. Perhaps she'd had a near-miss with a car . . . By morning, she'd be herself again.

I was getting a whisky when it occurred to me there might be other cats hiding in the house. A careful search revealed the three little ones in the back of my tool-cupboard, a huddle of mindless terror, quite impervious to the sharp edges of the saws and chisels they were crouching on.

They couldn't all have had near-misses. Something was terrifying them. It made the bolted doors and curtained windows seem pretty thin. I wished Rama was here. Rama wouldn't frighten so easy. But of Rama there was no sign, even in the draughty attics.

I had an absurd desire to call Sergeant Watkinson. But what about? It was gone eleven, and the world was away, asleep. It wouldn't want to know about my problems, at least till morning. Self-help, Howard, self-help! I went up to Peter's room, to get the rifle. Again, the oily smell of cartridges reminded me of happier days. Would they still work, after ten years? Though God knew what I intended to shoot that night. Only, *I* wasn't giving up my eyes without a struggle.

I made up a big fire in the lounge; pushed furniture against the windows, with some absurd idea of tripping up anything that tried to come through them. Settled in my armchair with another, very small whisky. Didn't want my wits fuddled. I tried playing some Bach on the record-player; but the sound blocked out all other noise and I switched off quickly again. I finally settled with the gun across my knee, the lantern beside me in case the lights went out, and *The Lord of the Rings* balanced across the gun. But Frodo's journey – my favourite passage in all literature – was no comfort. I was listening, listening, checking each noise as it came. A hunted animal in its lair, but at least an animal with some teeth.

But we're not as good as animals at staying alert. Whether it was the whisky or the fire, I began to doze. Twice, the book falling from my lap brought me leaping awake. Once, it was the collapse of coals in the fire. Once, the grandfather-clock in the hall, chiming one, sounding as meaningless as it would to a cat.

And yet, in the end, my senses did not let me down. Suddenly, I came out of sleep wide-awake, not knowing what had wakened me. But I somehow knew this was it. I remember putting my book and whisky glass carefully on one side, out of harm's way; picking up the gun and pointing it at the white door of my lounge, and not forgetting to slip off the safety-catch.

188

At the back of the house, the cat-flap banged. Which of the little cats was moving? Or had Rama come home? I wasn't tempted to go and look; just kept sitting in my chair, pointing the rifle with fairly steady hands.

I never heard any footsteps; just the floorboards in the hall, creaking. Something heavier than a cat.

The door-handle rattled three times, as a cat will sometimes rattle it, wanting to be in. The third time, it began to turn, hesitantly, as if the creature wasn't used to opening doors. I had an awful temptation to shoot through the white door, just above the handle, to hear a heavy body fall, and know that I was safe. To kill what stood there, without having to look at it. But I'm a man, not an animal.

The door opened only two inches; a two-inch gap of darkness, and something taking stock of me, out of that darkness. I nudged up the barrel of the gun, to warn whatever stood there not to try my patience too long.

'Howard?' It was the voice from the signal-box.

At that moment, I realised I was still wearing my reading-spectacles, and everything more than two feet away was a blur. My outdoor-spectacles were on the table beside me, but to reach them, I'd have to take one hand off the gun.

The door swung open, and I thought I was going crazy.

Mrs Raven stood there in the shadows; Mrs Raven our cleaner, in her big-checked nylon overall.

'Mrs Raven,' I said, dumbfounded. 'What are *you* doing here?' I remember thinking, ridiculously, that this was Monday night – well, Tuesday morning – and

189

Mrs Raven came on Thursdays. Then the creature swam in from the shadows, and even wearing my reading-spectacles, I realised I wasn't talking to Mrs Raven, but something dressed in Mrs Raven's overall. That always hung on the back door, above the cat-flap.

Where Mrs Raven's headscarf usually hid her curlers, flamed a mane of burning red hair. Where Mrs Raven's wrinkled grey stockings covered a pair of spindle-shanks ... the overall, which enclosed Mrs Raven like a voluminous sack, was no more than a mini-dress on this thing.

She flowed in like a wave of grace, filling the room. She'd have flowed right over me, but I raised the small mean barrel of the gun.

That stopped her; whatever she was, she knew what a gun was for.

She curled herself smoothly down into my wife's chair, across the fireside. Without human modesty; so I was glad I was wearing my reading spectacles. All her body-hair seemed that same flaming red. She made my wife's chair look small; she made the room feel small; and it's not a small room. I wondered again about changing my spectacles but she'd be across the hearthrug in a flash, if I took my eyes off her.

'Howard?'

I peered. Got a blurred impression of large green eyes and, when she yawned, very white teeth. She was no more humanly modest with her yawn than with her body. Just yawned enjoyably to the fullest extent, without putting her hand over her mouth.

'You do know me, Howard.' She tried to stretch again; but the nylon overall was a constricting torment

190

to her. She put up a hand and the nylon ripped open, as if it were paper. From the sound, I could imagine the size of her fingernails.

'You remind me . . . of my cat Rama,' I said, forcing a laugh; not wanting to be totally outfaced. It seemed a good brave thing to laugh at such a monster.

'I *am* your cat Rama.'

Then I knew I was asleep and dreaming. The dreams of a lonely fifty-year-old, whose wife has been away too long. But a man must act in his dreams as he would act in life. Or else he is a hypocrite. So I kept the dream-gun pointing at her.

'If you are my cat Rama, you will behave like my cat Rama. At least while you are in *my* house. What you do outside is your own business.'

I jumped awake to the rattle of the cat-flap, to find I was in a cold and empty room. No wonder the room was so cold; the draught had swung the door open two inches . . .

I didn't stir from my chair for the rest of the night, though I made the fire up several times, and dozed till daylight. Some dreams can leave a heavier impression on you than reality. I wakened finally with bright early sunshine making streaks across the darkened hearthrug. I pulled back the curtains, feeling a total fool, with a very stiff neck as a memento of my foolishness. The book, the gun and the whisky glass were not a welcome sight.

I checked the house; every door and window was, of course, locked and secure. My five cats gave me their usual sleepy, stretching greeting when I entered the kitchen. I had to stroke their heads in turn; Rama first of course. I tried staring her out; and failed as usual. Otherwise she seemed perfectly normal. I felt a certain reluctance to touch her at all; but made myself. I am not the kind of person who blames a cat for my own silly dreams. Nevertheless, from that day there was a coldness, a distance between us.

Mrs Raven's overall hung on the door as usual. Except that when I turned it round, all the buttons were missing, and seemed to have been removed with unnecessary force. I found them in the pocket. That seemed a little odd, but then I'd never taken any interest in the garment before. Perhaps my wife, or Mrs Raven were busily engaged in taking it in, or letting it out, or some other mysterious thing that women seem always to be doing to garments. Certainly the overall wasn't seriously damaged. Nothing Mrs Raven couldn't put right in ten minutes. I made a resolve to ask her about it, but forgot and never did.

Life continued much as before; except that Rama seemed to get ever bigger and sleeker, and I felt an increasing reluctance to join my family in Scotland for Christmas, and leave Mrs Raven and Rama to each other's tender mercies.

But Christmas was still ten days off when it happened. I was buying my supper in the village off-licence, when I heard about it. A young girl on her way home alone from a Christmas dance the previous night, had been dragged into the old works and murdered.

'I saw the young copper who found her,' said the woman behind the counter, her eyes wide upon the horror of some inward scene. 'I had to give him a cup of tea, he was that shaken. He was sick all over our bathroom floor. He said it was like a wild beast had mauled her to death . . .'

I just stood there, with my cold Cornish pasties in my hand, afraid I was going to drop them. I remember, there was a young man standing opposite me in the queue. A small young man in a black leather jacket, a workman of some kind, because he had a bag of tools in his hand, with the handle of a hammer and the point of a screwdriver sticking out. He kept staring at the woman and then staring at me, drinking in our faces, and I remember thinking he knows something, he knows about me and about Rama. I heard no more; I was only too eager to get out of the shop without disgracing myself.

When I got home, Rama was nowhere to be seen. Sergeant Watkinson rang the bell, as I was sitting in the cold kitchen, staring blankly at the pages of an old colour supplement.

I couldn't help glancing at Rama's usual chair as I showed him it.

'Something missing, sir?'

'No, no,' I said, elaborately counting the four cats that remained. 'Four – all accounted for.'

'The other one never turned up, then?'

I shook my head. He'd never believe any of it, anyway. Besides, this was between me and Rama.

He asked if I'd heard anything the previous night. Living in the house nearest the old works . . . I shook my head with conviction. That much was true. I asked about the girl's injuries. He just shook his head. Nothing was being released.

When he'd gone, I went to Peter's room and took down the rifle.

The next week was hell. The gun was always ready, but there was no sign of her. The other cats began to eat her food, sleep in her chair. I don't know how I got through school. In the evenings, I drank. My wife sensed my mood over the phone; threatened to come home. I managed to put her off.

Then, the night before the end of term, I looked up at the uncurtained window (I no longer bothered to draw the curtains) and saw her great cat-mask peering at me. I wasn't frightened; only in despair that she would vanish like a ghost before I could fetch the gun.

But when I returned, she was still there, staring in calmly, sadly, almost, I would have said, lovingly. I fumbled with the safety catch, raised the rifle to shoot her through the glass, and her head immediately vanished.

I ran outside into a clear moonlit night. She stood on top of the yard-gate, silvered by the moon. I raised the rifle, and again she dropped out of sight.

I ran after her, like a mad thing, in my shirtsleeves. Saw her streaking down the grass slopes to the old works, far ahead, too difficult a shot by moonlight. I ran without hope, then. She would lose me in the works, easily; be crouched on a girder, six feet above my head, and I'd never notice.

But when I reached the works she was visible, a pale streak trotting along the main soda-pipe. I began to suspect she was playing with me, as if I was a mouse. Leading me to what? Her death? My death? I no longer cared. My middle-aged breath scraped harshly in my throat, tasting foully of whisky and despair.

Half an hour later, on the slope to Brinkton Woods, I knew she was leading me on. Letting me draw nearer and nearer, yet always on the move; never giving me the chance of a straight shot.

Then, in the depths of the wood, she vanished. I sat on a fallen tree, sweating and gasping and wishing I was dead. Brinkton Woods is for lovers, not cats and crazy middle-aged men. I felt too weak to walk two miles home. Why had she *done* this to me? I didn't care if she killed me.

So why did I start up in fright, at a crashing in the nearby bushes? It didn't sound like Rama anyway; much too noisy and disorganised.

Then a young girl screamed.

An ugly sound; a thud on flesh. Then the scream turned into a sobbing, a wild sobbing of sheer disbelief.

'Oh no, oh no, oh no, please don't, please don't.'

Another ugly noise, before it got into my thick skull that the girl might be being murdered. I'd never heard the sound of a killing before; it doesn't sound like you expect it to sound, from the telly.

I slipped off the safety-catch and ran. Oh, Rama!

I burst through the bushes, into a tiny clearing where the moonlight lay full. A girl lay on her back, skirt up round her waist, pale silken legs thrashing wildly while something dark crouched with horrible intentness over her head and neck.

As I raised the rifle, uncertain of getting in a shot, wondering whether to leap in and use it like a club, the girl gave one last desperate upward push with her bleeding arms. Just for a second, the dark shape hung above her, quite separate . . .

I fired at the centre of the rib-cage. No animal can do much harm once you've hit it in the rib-cage, even if you don't find the heart.

I was too close to miss, even by moonlight. The beast fell sideways, pivoting on the girl's outstretched arms, and lay quite still.

'Goodbye, Rama,' I mouthed bitterly, and walked across. The girl mustn't have been hurt too badly. She had leapt to her feet and began screaming again for all she was worth. Perhaps she thought I was the Second Murderer.

The beast had rolled into the shadow of a bush. I pushed it with my foot, still covering it with the rifle.

It was a man.

A small dark man in a black leather jacket. A bag of tools lay beside him; hammer and screwdriver. He was quite dead; a small damp warm patch where his heart would be.

A feeling of being watched made me look up. Rising above the bush was a head, with two great dark sorrowful eyes, and a mane of hair that managed to look red even in the moonlight.

Rama raised one hand.

'Goodbye, Howard.' It had sadness and longing and contempt in it.

Then Rama was gone, forever.

Robert Westall
The Devil on the Road

A breeze blew, the gibbet creaked again. And then the smell hit me . . .

Caught in a freak storm, John Webster and his motorbike need shelter. Down a rough track he finds an old building with symbols carved in the doors. And a friendly animal presence, luring him towards the unknown . . .

There is something very odd going on in Vaser's Barn. But by the time John stops pretending it's just a cosy place to stay, it's too late. The evils from its past demand another victim.

A brilliant supernatural thriller from master storyteller Robert Westall.

Robert Westall
The Machine-Gunners

*'Some bright kid's got a gun and 2000 rounds of live ammo.
And that gun's no peashooter. It'll go through a brick wall at a
quarter of a mile.'*

Chas McGill has the second-best collection of war souvenirs
in Garmouth, and he desperately wants it to be the best.
When he stumbles across the remains of a German bomber
crashed in the woods – its shiny, black machine-gun still
intact – he grabs his chance. Soon he's masterminding his
own war effort, with dangerous and unexpected results . . .

'. . . not just the best book so far written for children about
the Second World War, but also a metaphor for now.'
Times Literary Supplement

'No better junior novel than this has appeared for a long
time . . . Indeed, adult readers would learn a great deal
from it.'
The School Librarian

WINNER OF THE CARNEGIE MEDAL

Robert Westall titles
available from Macmillan

The prices shown below are correct at the time of going to press.
However, Macmillan Publishers reserve the right to show new retail
prices on covers which may differ from those previously advertised.

ROBERT WESTALL

Blitzcat	0 330 31040 2	£3.99
The Cats of Seroster	0 330 29239 0	£3.99
Fathom Five	0 330 32230 3	£3.99
The Machine-Gunners	0 330 33428 X	£3.99
A Time of Fire	0 330 33754 8	£3.99
The Haunting of Chas McGill	0 330 34065 4	£3.99
The Watch House	0 330 33571 5	£3.99
The Devil on the Road	0 330 34064 6	£3.99
Ghosts and Journeys	0 330 30904 8	£3.99
A Place for Me	0 330 33427 1	£3.99
The Promise	0 330 31741 5	£3.99
Rachel and the Angel	0 330 30235 3	£3.99
Voices in the Wind	0 330 35218 0	£3.99
The Wind Eye	0 330 32234 6	£3.99
Yaxley's Cat	0 330 32499 3	£3.99

All Macmillan titles can be ordered at your local bookshop
or are available by post from:

**Book Service by Post
PO Box 29, Douglas, Isle of Man IM99 1BQ**

Credit cards accepted. For details:
Telephone: 01624 675137
Fax: 01624 670923
E-mail: bookshop@enterprise.net

Free postage and packing in the UK.
Overseas customers: add £1 per book (paperback)
and £3 per book (hardback).